Dedication

To Melissa Brown...

You have been with me from the very beginning, talked me off more ledges than I can count and stopped me from deleting every single book no less than four times.

Thank you for all of your support, encouragement and guidance.

I would be completely lost without you.

And I do NOT say this with scorn. ;)

Chapter 1

BRODY

"GOOD MORNING," KACIE SAID IN a soft, sexy tone. My eyes stayed glued shut but I felt her scoot over and snuggle into my side. I tucked my arm under her and pulled her tight against me.

"Are you gonna wake up?" she asked after a minute, swirling her fingertips around on my chest.

"No," I answered, still refusing to open my eyes.

"Brody!" she said playfully, poking me over and over.

"Do I have to?"

"Kinda. The girls will be barging through that door any second asking about the tree. We promised them we'd go get it today, remember?"

I groaned, not wanting to wake up yet. "What time is it?"

"A little after seven."

"Seven?! Kacie, my tryptophan hasn't even worn off yet from yesterday. Let me stay in my turkey coma for a little bit longer."

She trailed a few tiny kisses along my shoulder. "You're

1

leaving first thing tomorrow morning. Let's not waste the whole morning sleeping."

A wicked grin crept across my lips as I cracked one eye open and peeked down at her. "You're right. Sleeping is lame. I can think of a much better way to waste the morning." As I started to roll over on top of her, our bedroom door flew open, the doorknob banging hard against the wall. "Or not." I sighed and fell back on the bed.

"Can we leave now?" Emma exclaimed, charging toward us like a rhino.

Kacie sat up quickly. "Emma! Shhhh! You're gonna wake your sisters."

"Too late," Piper said dryly as she walked into the room with her eyes barely open. Lucy followed right behind her, yawning as she carried Grace in her arms. They all plopped down on the foot of the bed as Emma shot us an innocent grin and shrugged.

"Okay, well, how about we have some breakfast, then we'll go get the tree?" Kacie asked, just as Grace broke free from Piper's arms and sprinted across the bed and threw herself into Kacie's lap.

"I was thinking about something," I said. "You know how yesterday you mentioned, like four hundred times, how you want this year to be the most perfect Christmas ever?"

A small, embarrassed smile spread across her lips. "Yeah?"

"Well, what if instead of getting our tree from the Boy Scout lot like we always do, we head back to Sullivan's Tree Farm? Ya know . . . take the big tractor out, pick the perfect one and cut it down ourselves?"

Emma's mouth dropped open and her eyes widened. "Really? Can we, Mom?"

"Yeah, can we?" Piper added excitedly.

Kacie pressed her lips together, looking at each of the girls and back down at me. "We haven't done that since the twins were little."

I nodded. "Exactly."

"Let's do it!" she said with a big grin, her green eyes sparkling. "We'll have breakfast, then bundle up and go get the perfect tree to go with our perfect Christmas."

Emma threw her arms up in the air in celebration as Piper jumped off the bed and danced around.

"Ooooh—" Piper froze suddenly and slid her eyes over to Kacie, "—can you make the perfect blueberry muffins for a perfect breakfast?"

Emma nodded in agreement and stuck out her bottom lip, giving her mom puppy dog eyes.

"I could go for blueberry muffins too," Lucy mumbled into the quilt without lifting her head.

"Okay then. Muffins it is," Kacie said with a giggle. She turned and looked down at me with soft, sincere eyes. "Thanks for suggesting the tree farm thing."

I shrugged, returning her smile. "Sounds like a fun day with my five favorite girls." She grinned back at me, crinkling her nose up just the way I liked it. I tucked a piece of hair that had escaped her messy ponytail behind her ear. "You're kinda cute first thing in the morning, you know that?"

Her eyebrows shot up. "Am I?"

"Yeah, you are. Come here." I grabbed the sleeve of her pajamas and pulled her toward me. She leaned down and gently put her lips on mine.

"Ewwww!" Piper called out. "They're doing it again!"

Kacie cracked a smile against my mouth, but didn't move.

"Seriously," Lucy groaned. "You two are so gross!"

They both made gagging noises as they hopped off the bed and hurried out of the room, Emma trailing right behind them. Kacie pulled back and shook her head. "One day they're going to appreciate how much we love each other."

"That might be true, but I doubt they'll ever appreciate how much we make out." I laughed and rubbed her back.

A little while later, with bellies full of blueberry muffin and yogurt, we closed the door behind us and were on our way to the tree farm. Rocks crunched under the tires as we pulled into the parking lot.

"Wow! It's crowded." Kacie said, looking out the window.

I shrugged. "I'm not surprised . . . it's the day after Thanksgiving *and* the weather is nice today. All I'm saying is they better have some of those donuts or I'm gonna turn into the Hulk and start pulling trees out of the ground with my bare hands."

Kacie rolled her eyes and shook her head.

"Ooooh, I remember those donuts," Piper said from the backseat.

"Yeah!" Lucy agreed. "They were huge and warm and soft and cinnamony."

Kacie turned from the window and looked straight at me with a funny look on her face. "And last time we were here, Brody ate all of them. Remember that too?"

Lucy and Piper laughed in unison as I pulled the SUV into the first parking space I found. The girls sprang from the car, clearly eager to pick out a tree. As we made our way to the cabin, they chattered excitedly about what kind of tree they wanted.

"I want a tall one," Lucy said.

Piper shook her head as she spread her arms far apart. "No, let's do a really, really fat one. The tall ones are too hard to put the ornaments on."

"That's what we have Brody for!" Lucy laughed, peeking back at me.

"Really?" I teased. "You only keep me around to hang the ornaments on the top of the tree?"

"Pretty much," Lucy joked.

"Not me." Kacie wrapped her arm around my waist and squeezed. "I keep you around for *lots* of reasons."

Her sexy little smirk was an invite I could not turn down. I dipped my head and put my lips gently against hers.

"Seriously?" Piper squealed as she rolled her eyes and walked faster. "Oh my God! Can you at least not do it when you're with us?"

Kacie let out a small giggle and pulled back quickly. "Fine. No kissing in public."

"Thank God," Lucy groaned.

As soon as we walked through the door to the huge, weathered red barn that served as the warming house for cookies and hot chocolate, the smell of cinnamon and sugar filled the air. Lucy, Piper, Emma and Kacie all closed their eyes and inhaled deeply with tiny smiles on their faces.

"Can I help you?" a cheerful voice asked.

We turned to see a young woman with a warm smile standing behind us. She looked from Kacie to me and her mouth dropped open. "You. You're Brody Murphy!"

I returned her smile with a nod. "I am."

Her hands flew up to her mouth. "Oh my God. You're *you!* I'm a huge hockey fan. Huge, huge hockey fan! I can't believe you're standing in my barn!" She dropped her hands and continued rambling. "Well, not *my* barn—it's my mom's barn— her name is Barb. She's a Wild fan too. I can't wait to tell her you were here. Sorry, I'm a little excited." She finally stopped talking and took a breath, a nervous grin still plastered to her face.

I snuck a quick glance at her name badge. "Hi, Kerrie." I held my hand out to her.

"Oh my God, you said my name." Her hand trembled as she shook mine back. "This is the best day ever. Can I have your autograph?"

"Of course!" I said, gently pushing Grace's stroller toward Kacie.

Kerrie hurried around the wooden counter and pulled out a

piece of plain paper. "Here, sign this. Write anything."

I took the pen from her still-shaking hand and started writing.

SULLIVAN'S TREE FARM HAS THE BEST DONUTS!

BRODY MURPHY
#30

Kerrie peeked down at the piece of paper and started giggling way harder than my note deserved. "Oh my God. You are *too* funny! I'll tell you what. You guys go out and find the perfect tree and while you're gone, I'll fix you up a warm batch of your very own donuts. Maybe even one to take home too."

"Deal!"

"We normally put twelve people on a wagon, but do you guys want your own?" she continued.

I glanced back at Kacie, who was nodding enthusiastically, then back at Kerrie. "That would be awesome. Thank you!"

"Sure thing. Just give me a minute." She pulled a walkie-talkie out of her back pocket and started talking into it as I turned and stepped back to Kacie.

"Since I started playing hockey, I've gotten tables at the best restaurants, tickets to sold out games and shows, hell . . . I even got a free car once, but I can honestly say having a fresh batch of donuts made for me might just be the best perk yet."

Kacie laughed and shook her head. "I think the fact that it's getting us a private wagon to go out and find our tree is my favorite perk." She looked up at me and blinked a couple times. "What an amazing start to the perfect Christmas."

I put my hand around the back of her neck and pulled her

against me. "What's with this perfect Christmas thing, Kacie? You keep mentioning it."

"Can we go over there and look at the ornaments?" Lucy interrupted, pointing her thumb toward the Christmas Shoppe in the corner.

"Sure," Kacie nodded. "But look with your eyes. No touching. Got it?"

Lucy, Piper, and Emma nodded and ran off.

Kacie bent down and unzipped Grace's coat a little bit near the collar. As usual, she'd fallen sound asleep the minute we put her in the stroller, but it was warm in the barn and her upper lip had started to sweat.

"Are you ignoring my question?" I asked.

"No," she shook her head before letting out a heavy sigh. "I don't know. You know that Christmas has always been my favorite holiday, but I'm feeling more nostalgic this year for some reason. I don't know if it's because I turned thirty, because the girls are in their last year before middle school, or what . . . but I'm just feeling like life is too short and I want an amazing Christmas."

I nodded slowly. "I get it . . . and I agree. Life is moving too damn fast lately and I want to slow it down too."

Her eyes dropped. "Part of me feels like this is the last year that Lucy and Piper are still little, ya know? Pretty soon we'll be dealing with mean girls, pushy boys, and periods."

A chill bolted down my spine and I shuddered.

She looked at me curiously. "What was that for?"

"That. All of that."

"Brody, we have four daughters. You're going to have to deal with those things eventually. Especially hormones and periods."

My eyes bulged in horror and I crammed my fingers in my ears. "La, la, la, la, la, la, la."

Kacie grabbed my forearms and tugged on them. "Knock it off, you big baby. Periods aren't that big of a deal."

"For you! You have a uterus!"

She smacked my chest as she looked around, "First of all . . . lower your voice. Second, be serious with me. You might *really* have to deal with this someday."

I stared at her for a second, desperately trying to find an escape hatch to our conversation. "I'm definitely *not* dealing with periods."

"You might not have a choice." She shrugged. "What if I'm not home when they get it for the first time?"

Panic shot like lightning bolts through different parts of my body.

She waved her hand in front of my face. "Hello? Earth to Brody?"

"Well," I finally said, "that's easy. I'll stick them in the bathtub and call you to come home immediately from wherever you are."

"The bathtub?!" she exclaimed dramatically. "Brody, you *cannot* put them in the bathtub."

"Sure I can," I joked with a shrug. "Dads are for beating up boys, moms are for periods. I think I read that in a book somewhere, so that makes it official."

Kacie shook her head, letting out a heavy sigh. "What am I going to do with you?"

I couldn't stop the mischievous grin that instantly formed on my lips. "Well, we *are* in a barn and I know what barns do to you, so . . . there's an idea."

Chapter 2

Kacie

I GOT UP EARLY THE next morning to see Brody out the door for his road trip. He was only going to be gone a couple of days, but I never let him leave without walking him to the door and kissing him good-bye. Shortly after he left, the girls got up and were sniffing around the kitchen, trying to find something for breakfast.

"What do you guys want me to make you?" I asked through a yawn.

Piper shrugged.

"You know what sounds good?" Lucy asked in a dreamy tone. "Breakfast at Gigi's."

I tilted my head to the side and pressed my lips together, thinking about her proposal. I was beyond exhausted and the thought of my mom making breakfast for the five of us was more than a little appealing. "That *does* sound good, doesn't it? Let's go!"

"Yessssssss!" Lucy hissed, pumping her fist in the air.

"Should we change?" Piper asked.

"Uh . . ." I stammered, looking down at each of them, still in their pajamas. "You know what . . . no. We'll drive over today. Everybody in the car!"

My mom lived less than a hundred yards away, through a small patch of woods. We typically walked through the path, but given our current outfits, a car ride seemed more fitting.

The girls giggled the whole twenty-second ride over to my mom's and, as I pulled up to her inn, they jumped out of the car and sprinted up the wooden steps.

"Look at all you adorable little ragamuffins," I heard my mom say as I took Grace out of her car seat. I propped her on my hip as I climbed the steps too.

"Morning, Mom."

"Hi, sweetheart." As I got closer, she scrunched her eyebrows together. "You look like hell."

"Thanks," I said with a laugh. "I *feel* like hell. It was a looooooong day yesterday."

She reached out and took Grace from me. "Well, come on in and I'll make you all breakfast while you tell me about it."

As I plopped down at the island, the girls ran down the hall to my old bedroom that my mom had turned into a playroom.

"Did Brody leave?" Mom asked as she opened the fridge and pulled out two cartons of eggs.

"Yeah, a little while ago." I rested my elbow on the counter and my chin in my palm.

"Did you guys pick out a tree?"

"Yep. It took forever. I swear we walked the whole property three times before we found one we all agreed on, then when we got it home we needed to open it and let it sit for a while so we baked cookies." I reached into the bowl of grapes she had on the island and popped one in my mouth. "So after all that, they decorated the tree, completely trashing my family room in the process, and we put them to bed. Then Brody and I cleaned up the kitchen and family room before we finally went up to bed ourselves."

Mom turned and stared at me with wide eyes. "I'm exhausted just listening to all that."

"Don't get me wrong, it was a great day, just a long one." I yawned again.

"After breakfast, why don't you leave the fab four here and go home for a quick nap?" She asked as she started cracking eggs and dropping them in a bowl.

"Thanks for the offer, but I promised them we'd watch a few Christmas movies today, so that's our plan."

She grabbed a whisk and started whipping the eggs quickly. "You're a good mom, Kacie. Trees . . . cookies . . . movies . . . It's gotta be hard doing all that when Brody is gone so much."

I shrugged and grabbed a couple more grapes. "It can be, but we're used to it at this point. Wait—" I sat up and looked over to her family room, "—speaking of trees, where's your tree? You always put it up the day after Thanksgiving, like us."

"I'm just a little slow this year." She poured the eggs into the frying pan and grabbed a spatula. "Fred and I were lazy yesterday. We stayed in bed most of the day and watched HGTV."

"I heard my name . . . you better be saying good things," Fred teased as he came around the corner, smiling at me with a broom in his hand. "Hi, sweetheart." He bent down and kissed the side of my head. "Where are all those crazy girls of yours?"

I motioned toward the hall. "Destroying the playroom."

He nodded with a quick chuckle. "I'll go say hi in a minute after I finish sweeping the front porch."

"You want breakfast?" Mom asked, glancing over at him.

He stopped in the doorway. "Maybe. Whatcha making?"

"Eggs. Bacon. Sausage. Fruit."

"I'll take all of the above," he said as he walked across the room and planted a kiss on her cheek. "Be back in a bit."

A minute later the front door closed with a thud, and I stared at my mom who was still smiling to herself like a love-struck teenager.

"You two are ridiculously adorable, you know that?" I finally said.

She looked back at me quickly, then returned her attention to the pan of crackling bacon on the stove. "He's so great, Kacie."

"He is," I agreed. "You're a lucky woman."

Turning to face me, she pinched her lips together and crossed her arms over her chest. "We both are."

I nodded, suddenly missing Brody more than usual. "For sure."

"Alright . . . go get those girls so they can eat while everything is still hot. I'm gonna set the table."

I hopped off the stool and quietly made my way down the hall, hoping to hear whatever it was the girls were saying.

"You *know* Santa?" Emma said in a surprised tone just as I got to the door.

"Yep," Piper responded. "We met him a long time ago, when we were your age, and we've been friends ever since."

Leaning in carefully toward the door, I prayed the wood boards beneath my feet didn't creak and give me away.

Emma continued excitedly, "And you can write to him?!"

"Shhh!" Piper hissed. "Yes, I told you . . . we have his real address and can write to him, but you can't tell anyone, because if adults find out, he cancels Christmas and no one gets anything. Got it?"

I didn't hear Emma answer, but I could just picture her standing there wide-eyed, nodding at her big sister's little white lie.

"So, you tell us what you want, and every time you clean our room, or do what we say, we'll write to him and tell him to get you one of those things for sure. Deal?"

That little shit.

"Uh huh," Emma agreed innocently.

"Good. Now remember . . . don't tell anyone. Promise?"

"Pinky promise," Emma answered eagerly.

I raised my fist and knocked on the door. "Girls . . . breakfast," I called out, deciding I'd deal with Piper and her antics later.

They followed me down the hall, like little ducklings waddling behind their mother, and hopped up around the table. I buckled Grace into her high chair and walked over to help mom carry the bowls of food to the table. We scooped piles of scrambled eggs, bacon, and strawberries onto their plates and they started shoveling the food into their mouths.

"Slow down," I said to Grace, who was eating the strawberries as fast as I could cut them. She grinned up at me with piece of egg stuck to the corner of her mouth. I bent down and kissed the top of her sweet head.

"Gigi, where's your Christmas tree?" Emma asked in between bites.

Mom let out a soft sigh. "I haven't put it up yet, sweetheart."

Emma's eyes grew wide. "Can we help you with it?"

"Uh . . . maybe," Mom stammered, her eyes darting from each of the girls to me as she shifted uncomfortably. I tilted my head and frowned at her before she looked away.

The girls finished their breakfast in record time and hurried back down the hall to the playroom.

"Ah, ah, ah!" I called out. "Piper, come back here, please."

She spun around.

"Can you clear the plates from the table and wipe it down for me?"

"What? Why me?" she complained as she walked over and started balling up the paper napkins.

"I'll tell you what—" I smirked as I stole a quick glance down the hall to make sure no other kids were in earshot, "—you do this for me and I'll write a letter to my friend, Santa, telling him all about how amazing you are. Maybe he'll bring you something you want for sure."

She froze and looked up at me but didn't say anything. Her cheeks turned pinker by the second.

"Busted," I said, crossing my arms over my chest. "Now . . . you're going to help clean up breakfast, then you're going to stop trying to bribe your sister to do your chores, got it?"

She nodded and quietly cleaned up most of the kitchen table. After a minute, I stepped in and helped her with the rest. Before she left the room, she turned and wrapped her arms around my waist. "Sorry, Mom."

"You're her big sister, Piper. Her role model. Be nice, okay?" I said through a sigh.

Her head nodded against my chest and she skipped down the hall.

My mom snickered from the sink.

"Are you laughing?" I asked incredulously.

"Just a little," she answered.

I let out my own small laugh and shook my head as I sat back down at the island. "I'm telling you, Mom, that one is going to be the death of me."

Mom set the plates down in the sink and turned to face me. "Baby, I said that same thing about you at least a hundred times."

I stuck my tongue out at her playfully and glanced down at my phone. "Okay. It's almost eleven. I'm gonna take the girls home so we can all get dressed and brush our teeth and stuff. Then I'll come back and we'll do your tree together?"

Her eyes pinched shut and she rubbed her forehead with her fingertips. Mom and I were close and I could tell when she had something on her mind. Whatever it was . . . it was huge. "Kacie," she finally said. "I have to talk to you about something."

"Okay . . ." I said slowly, nervous to hear whatever it was that had obviously been bugging her all morning.

"I don't even know how to say this because it's going to upset you and I don't want to upset you, but you're going to be upset," she rambled, anxiously wringing her fingers together as she dropped her eyes to the floor.

"Mom, you're freaking me out. What is it?"

She took a long, deep breath and lifted her eyes to mine. "Honey, we're selling the inn."

"Wait . . . what?" I said, sure that I heard her wrong.

"We've been thinking about it for a while. Fred and I aren't getting any younger and it's just getting to be too much to keep up with," she explained, taking a step closer to me.

I sat stunned, not sure how, or whether I even wanted to, process what she was telling me. The inn was my life. My second home. I couldn't imagine not being able to walk over and sit at the island anytime I wanted, or sit on the deck and watch the girls play in the garden with Gigi while Fred tinkered in the garage, or sit on the end of the pier with Brody and talk about everything and nothing.

"Mom, you can't sell the inn," I blurted out.

"Kacie—"

"No." I jumped up and started pacing back and forth across the kitchen. "I'm serious. Ninety percent of my life's memories are in this house. The twins practically grew up here. You can't sell it. I won't let you."

"Kacie—"

"We'll buy it!" I interrupted again. "Brody and me . . . we'll buy it. How much are you going to sell it for? We'll give you whatever you want for it."

"Kacie!" she hollered in an attempt to stop my incoherent rambling. I froze and stared at her as her face softened and she continued, "Honey, we've already accepted an offer."

I pulled my brows in tight as I sunk back onto the stool. "What? How?" I said in a calm, even, sad tone.

She sat down on the stool next to me and gently put her hands on mine. "We decided to put the inn on the market a few weeks ago, but before we could even get the sign in the ground, someone contacted our realtor and made an offer. A really good offer. One we couldn't turn down—so we didn't."

I stared down at our hands and tried to listen to her words, but all I could hear was the blood rushing through my ears.

"And let's be honest," she continued, "I could never sell it to you anyway. You have four daughters to take care of and a husband who's gone half the year. You really think you could run this old inn too?"

"Maybe," I mumbled stubbornly.

"Sweetheart, I love that you love this place, but it's time to move on." Her words stung. I felt like I was being told to move on from something I didn't even *want* to move on from. I wanted to go back in time fifteen minutes and have everything be normal again.

"When?" I asked after a minute, my voice cracking.

"Huh?"

Clearing my throat, I tried again. "When do you close?"

"Oh. Uh . . . right after the New Year. January fourth."

The front door slammed and Fred's familiar whistle got closer. "Sorry! After I swept the porch I raked the front yard real quick. Hope you guys didn't eat all the—" He stopped talking and looked at me. "Everything okay?"

Mom nodded. "I told her."

"Oh." His tone turned solemn.

I sniffed and tried to hold in the tears that had begun stinging the backs of my eyes. Fred walked up behind me and put his arm around my shoulders. "You okay?"

I shrugged and shook my head, but didn't lift my eyes from the island. "No."

"I know this is hard, but it'll all be okay. I promise." Mom said as she squeezed my hand.

16

Fred slid the box of tissues toward me.

"Is this why you're not putting up a tree?" I asked as I dabbed my nose.

"Kinda," she answered. "I just didn't see the point to go through all that extra work when we're going to be packing up the house anyway."

Packing the house up. Those words made everything inside of me hurt.

I pinched my lips together and nodded slowly as a tear slid down my cheek. "Where are you going to live?"

"Well," mom said with a sigh as her eyes moved over to Fred. "We actually found a really cute, little house. It's nothing fancy, but perfect for the two of us. Big garage for Fred, small garden area for me, and a big playroom for when the girls want to have sleepovers. Plus, a huge porch and walking distance to town. We're going to rent it for now just to make sure we like it, but if we do, the owner said he'd be willing to sell."

My chest ached. It felt like someone had walked up and punched me as hard as they could right in the sternum. It wasn't even *my* house to be sad about, yet I was. I was sad. So incredibly, unbelievably, astronomically sad.

"Sounds nice," I said dryly. I *wanted* to be excited for them— I really did—but it was too soon. I don't know that I'd ever get over the heartbreak of losing the inn.

Chapter 3

BRODY

THE MINUTE OUR PLANE TOUCHED down, I turned my phone back on like I always did, except this time it blew up like the Fourth of July.

"Uh oh . . . someone's in trouble," Viper teased, nodding toward my phone.

"Shut up." I punched him in the arm and stared back down at my phone, waiting for the dinging to stop and all the notifications to come through.

I had a handful of missed texts and calls, all from Kacie's number. A knot immediately formed in my throat as I dialed her back without reading the texts.

She answered quickly. "Hi," she said in a soft voice. She only said one word but I knew my wife better than anyone and I could tell she'd been crying.

"Hey, what's going on?" I slowed my pace, hanging back a bit behind Viper and the rest of the team as we made our way through the airport. We were scheduled for an afternoon practice at the rink, but the tone in Kacie's voice had me worried

I was going to be on a plane headed back home instead.

"I'm sorry I called and texted so many times. I just . . . wanted to talk to you so badly."

"Don't apologize . . . is everything okay?"

"Yes. No. I don't know." She sniffed into the phone. "We went over to mom's for breakfast after you left this morning, and she told me they sold the inn."

"They sold the inn?" I repeated, the shock raising my voice.

Viper spun around when he heard me. "Who? What? Sold the inn?"

I shook my head and held up a finger for him to wait a minute.

"Yep, they sold it," Kacie said. "I don't even know what to think. I've been crying all morning."

"Oh, honey. I'm so sorry."

"Brody, how can they do this? I mean, I know it's theirs and they can do whatever they want with it, but they're still young. It's too early to get rid of it." Her voice cracked and she started to cry again.

"Aw, Kacie. Don't cry. It kills me to hear you cry when I can't do anything to help."

"I'm just so deflated. I told the girls we'd watch movies and hang out all day but I don't even feel like it anymore."

"Did you tell them?"

A loud sigh filled the phone. "Yeah. I had to . . . they could tell I was upset."

I felt helpless. Kacie was upset but there really was nothing I could do to make the situation better. It *was* Fred and Sophia's inn and I knew how much work went into running that place, but I also knew how much that old place meant to Kacie.

"Did they say when it'll all be final?"

"Yeah, right after New Year."

"Wow. That's just a little over a month away. Pretty quick."

"I know. I feel like it's all happening so fast. And she's not even putting a tree up or decorating. Not only is it not going to be the perfect Christmas, Christmas is gonna suck."

Her words broke my heart. I was absolutely crazy about my wife, and one of the things I loved most about her was the way she got overly excited about everything . . . like Christmas. I teased her about the perfect Christmas thing, but I really thought it was adorable. We walked through the door to the pick up area, the smell of exhaust fumes attacking my lungs as we walked toward our charter bus.

"Babe, I'm so sorry, but we're about to get on the bus and head over to the hotel to drop off our luggage, then we're going straight to the rink. Can I call you after practice?"

"Yeah." She sniffed one more time. "Just call me later when you get back. Hopefully I'll be in a better mood by then."

I felt bad getting off the phone with her, but listening to her cry while I was on the bus with thirty other guys wasn't a good idea. "Okay. I love you, Kacie."

"I love you too." She hung up and I shoved my phone in my back pocket.

"What the hell is going on?" Viper asked, eying me with a concerned look on his face.

I stepped up onto the bus and followed him all the way to the back. "I don't really know. I guess Sophia is selling the inn," I said as we sat down.

I stared straight ahead, still stunned by the news Kacie had just given me.

"Whoa. That's a big deal," Viper said, his voice as serious as I'd ever heard.

"I know. Kacie is pretty broken up over it."

Viper and I were quiet the whole way to the hotel. I think he was just as surprised as I was, and maybe even a little sad himself about the news. We'd all spent so much time hanging out at the inn. Even after Kacie and I built our own house, Sophia often had the whole gang over for chili on a cold Sunday in the winter when we were in town, or she'd host a huge barbecue in the summer and invite all of our friends and their kids to come and stay for the whole weekend. The Cranberry Inn belonged to all of us and it was going to be a huge loss, but Kacie would definitely feel the brunt of it. She lived there since she was a kid, long before I even came along. This was going to be so hard for her.

"Hey." Viper nudged me hard. "We're here."

I looked out the window and realized the bus had stopped and we were parked outside the hotel. I was so lost in my own mind that I hadn't even noticed.

I stood and flung my bag over my shoulder as Viper gave me a tight smile. "It sucks, man. Sorry."

I nodded and we headed inside. After we were all checked in, we left pretty quickly for practice. Viper made stupid jokes and tried to lift my mood on the way there, but none of it worked.

He reached over and smacked my leg. "Come on, man. Lighten up."

"I will as soon as we're on the ice. I need a distraction to work this all off and clear my head."

"What you need to do is spin this and make something good out of it," he said nonchalantly.

I turned and looked straight at him. "What . . . you get married and have a kid and suddenly you turn into an enlightened life coach?"

"Whatever, asshole. I'm serious." He rolled his eyes. "There has to be a way to make this easier on Kacie."

I shook my head. "I got nothin.'"

"Well, let's think about it." He turned and looked out the window, tapping his thumb against his knee. After a couple minutes I was convinced he'd forgotten what it was we were supposed to be thinking about, but he swung his head toward me. "She already sold the inn, right?"

"Uh . . . yeah. That's what Kacie said."

"Okay." He got a wild look in his eyes and turned in his seat to face me. "So that means there aren't any guests for the whole month of December . . . correct?"

I shrugged. "I would guess so. They probably wouldn't have people there while they're packing and stuff."

He clapped loudly. "Yes! Good! So . . . here's my thought. What if you talk to Kacie and invite everyone up there for one last week. Me, Michelle and the kids . . . Andy, Dani and their kids . . . maybe her friend Alexa? Oooh, Darla! She hasn't been home in a long time!"

My wheels started turning as fast as Viper was spitting out ideas. "What if I *didn't* tell Kacie and instead surprised her?"

He sat up straight and nodded slowly, his eyes wide. "Dude. You pull this off and you're going to get the blow job of a lifetime."

"But wait," I continued, ignoring him. "We have games. How's that gonna work?"

His shoulders dropped and he pressed his lips together, thinking hard. "Well . . . we have to go regardless of where the girls are, right?"

"Right."

"So instead of them sitting at their own houses, alone, they can just sit at the inn and hang out together, baking cookies, drinking wine and shit." He pulled out his phone and looked ahead at the schedule. "Oh. Bro, this is perfect. We're in Nashville on the twenty-second, St. Louis on the twenty-third, then we're home for three days."

"Wow," I peeked at the schedule over his shoulder.

My heart pounded wildly inside my chest and my mind raced with possibilities and scenarios as to how I could actually pull this plan off. I wanted so badly to save Kacie's perfect Christmas and, ironically, Viper's idea might be just that . . . perfect.

"I can't believe you, of all people, thought of *this*." I clamped my hand down hard on his shoulder and shook it.

"I know, right? And this might just be the first plan I've ever thought of that has zero chance of either of us ending up in jail for the night," he boasted. "We work well together, Murphy."

"That we do, Finkle. That we do."

"We should run for President and Vice President."

I narrowed my eyes and glared at him.

"What? I'm serious. Can you even imagine how much trouble we could get into running around the White House together?" He let out a loud laugh that made his shoulders shake.

"Viper . . ." I shook my head. "There is so much shit about you on the Internet that I don't think they'd even let you vote, let alone run for office."

"Give me a break," he rolled his eyes. "Did you see that last election? They let anyone run for President these days."

Practice flew by, mainly because the whole time my mind was at the inn instead of on the ice, like it should have been. Thankfully, Collins only glared a few times before I got my shit together enough to make it through practice. Once we got back to the hotel, I grabbed my phone and texted the one person I needed to make the whole plan even possible . . . Sophia.

> Hey. If Kacie is over there, do not tell her I'm texting you. If she is and you already said something, hurry up and lie. If she's not there, forget everything I said and call me.

Anxious as hell, I stared down at my phone, praying for it to ring. I was so excited about everything and I was dying to tell Sophia. Hopefully I hadn't screwed myself by texting her first. Finally, my phone rang and Sophia's number popped up.

"Hey!" I answered excitedly.

"Hey, yourself. Is everything okay?" Sophia asked.

"Yes. Well, yes and no. I talked to Kacie earlier."

"Oh," Sophia said. It was obvious by her tone that she knew exactly what I was talking about. "How was she?"

"Not the worst, but definitely not great. She was crying."

Sophia let out a soft sigh. "She was teary-eyed when she left here too. I feel awful, and that wasn't the way I wanted to tell her but it happened fast and I didn't really think things through."

"Sophia, I don't think it would have mattered how you told her. Kacie is more attached to that place than either of us realized and her reaction today was evidence of that. She would have been upset no matter what."

"You're probably right." She sounded sad too.

"That's actually why I called." My excitement echoed off the walls of the empty hotel room. "I have an idea. Actually—I take that back—Viper had an idea."

"Oh boy."

"I know. Usually his ideas are nothing but trouble, but this time he had a winner. You know how at Thanksgiving dinner Kacie kept talking about the perfect Christmas?"

"Yeah," Sophia said with a sigh. "Little chance of that happening now."

"Maybe not. So Viper suggested we have all of our friends to the inn to stay for a few days, or a week—whatever—kind of as one last hurrah at the inn type of thing . . . mixed with Christmas."

"Oh, wow. That's an amazing idea. *Viper* thought of that?"

"Yep."

"That's even more shocking." She laughed.

"And listen . . . I know it'll be hard with you trying to pack up and then us bringing people there, but if it helps, I'll hire a whole crew to come in the week after everyone leaves and pack everything for you."

"That's sweet of you, Brody, but it shouldn't be a problem. The guest rooms are pretty simple as it is, so it should be easy. I'm in. I'm totally in. We'll even decorate and put the trees up right before, just to add another layer to the surprise!"

"Sophia . . . I don't know what we'd do without you. You're the best."

"I *am* the best," she teased playfully. "Remember that when you shop for my Christmas present."

Chapter 4

Andy

I TOSSED MY KEYS ON my desk and stretched my arms high in the air. It had already been a chaotic morning at the office and it didn't appear my afternoon was going to be any calmer.

"Andy?" Dani stared down at a paper in her hand as she walked into my office. "I need you to look at something for me."

My eyes drifted down her body, admiring every sexy inch of her before I lifted them back to her face. "I'll look at anything you ask me to."

"It's this—" she froze and narrowed her dark eyes, glaring at me when she realized what I'd said. "Are you ever not horny?"

"When you're around? No." I answered honestly.

"Well, calm your boner for a minute, okay? I want your opinion on this offer from Under Armor." She walked over and set the papers on my desk.

"What is this?" I leaned over the papers and scanned them quickly.

"It's a shoe offer for Kyle Keegan from Under Armor. They

want to offer him his own cleat line, and it looks like a sound deal, but I just wanted you to take a peek real quick."

I raised my eyebrows and stood up straight. "Wow! This is impressive."

"Thanks." She shot me a bashful grin. "That kid's turning out to be a pretty big deal."

"Well, he's a talented kid." I sat down in my desk chair and crossed my arms over my chest. "Plus, he's got an amazing agent in his corner."

"I've got a pretty amazing agent in my corner too." Her shy smile returned. Dani was a spitfire . . . a confident, badass of a woman who didn't play coy often, but when she did, I found her even more irresistible than usual.

"Would you two cool it for like five minutes?" A loud voice boomed.

Both of our heads snapped toward the door.

"Hey! What are you doing here?" I walked toward a grinning Brody standing in my doorway.

"I was in the neighborhood and thought I'd stop by and say hi. Plus, I have to talk to you about something," he answered, shaking my hand back. He walked over and gave Dani a quick hug. "Good to see you too, Dani."

"Hey, Brody," she said as she hugged him back. "Alright, well, one of us needs to get some work done around here, so I'll let you two chat while I—"

"Actually wait—" Brody interrupted, "—what I have to ask him involves you too."

"Oh," she sounded surprised. "Okay."

He walked across the room and plopped down on the couch in the corner, propping his feet up on the coffee table. "So long story short, we found out the other day that Sophia is selling the inn."

My head jerked back a little. "The inn? You're kidding me."

He shook his head, "Unfortunately, I'm not kidding."

"Wow. How is Kacie doing with that?" I asked as Dani walked over and lifted her butt onto the corner of my desk.

Brody shrugged. "She was really sad when she found out, and she still is, but I think she's making peace with it a little bit. It was just really bad timing because she's going through this weird thing about her getting older and the girls getting older so she was hell bent on having the perfect Christmas . . . then she got this news."

"Yikes. That *is* bad timing," Dani said.

"Tell me about it," Brody said sarcastically. "So, anyway, here's where you guys come in. Viper had this idea—"

"Oh, shit," I said as I held my hand up, stopping him. "If it was Viper's idea, I don't want to hear it."

Brody laughed and rolled his eyes. "Believe it or not, he actually did good this time. He suggested I surprise Kacie with one last little party at the inn. Everyone brings their family and comes up for a few days and we do the whole friend Christmas thing. What do you think?"

I looked from Brody to Dani, who bit her lip and nodded at me excitedly.

"First of all, I think that our little Viper is growing up too fast, and second of all . . . we're totally in."

A huge grin broke out across Brody's face. "Awesome. We don't have exact dates yet, but I'm planning all that with Sophia right now, so I'll get back to you on it, if that's okay, but we're thinking a few days before Christmas to a few days after."

The phone on my desk rang out and I pushed the button, "Yes, Ellie."

"Sorry to bug you all, but Ms. Douglas' one o'clock is here."

"Oh, shit!" Dani hopped off my desk as she glanced down at her watch. "I totally forgot I had an appointment." She gave us both a quick wave and hurried out of the room.

"So wait—this all sounds great, but don't you and Viper have this little thing called hockey to worry about?" I linked my fingers together behind my head as I leaned back in my chair.

Brody grabbed the baseball off my coffee table and began flipping it up in the air. "We do, but the schedule totally works in our favor. We have two games a couple days before the Christmas break, and then we have the day after Christmas off too."

I pulled my bottom lip up a bit and nodded. "That does work out nicely. So you guys go do your thing and I'll hang back at the inn."

"Fuck that," Brody stopped flipping the ball and shook his head. "You're coming with us."

"On the road?"

"Yeah! Why not?"

I stared up at the ceiling as I tilted my head back and forth. "That could work. You'll have to get me the dates as soon as you can so I can have Ellie move things around and clear my schedule."

"Will do," Brody nodded. "Speaking of schedules . . . when is your wedding going on the calendar?"

I took a deep breath and puffed out my cheeks, exhaling slowly. "Who knows. We're both so damn busy, and the thought of shutting everything down for a week so we can get married and take a honeymoon is just . . . crazy."

"You guys should just go to Vegas like Viper and Michelle did."

"I thought about that but she's never been married before, so I want to do whatever she wants to do."

Brody arched an eyebrow, "Ya know . . . if you say the word, I'm sure Viper would get ordained on the Internet and marry you two in a heartbeat while you're up at the inn for Christmas."

As ridiculous as that sounded, it also sounded like a lot of fun. "That would be awesome, but I would never be able to keep a straight face with Viper acting all official. And like I said . . . it all comes down to what Dani wants. We've been so busy that we haven't talked about it much, but I think she kinda wants the white dress, flowers, the whole big thing and I have to give that to her. She deserves it."

"She does," he nodded in agreement. "With all she went through with Blaire, and then, of course, putting up with your ass every single day, that girl deserves a dream wedding."

"We were actually thinking maybe next summer when the kids are off school so we could take them on our honeymoon with us."

Brody's eyes zoned in on mine as he leaned forward, resting his elbows on his knees and locking his hands in front of him. "Wait a minute . . . you're taking your kids on your *honeymoon?* Uh . . . I think you've forgotten what's supposed to happen on a honeymoon, bro."

I let out a laugh. "I know it's not ideal, but I feel bad asking Gloria to keep them for an entire week, and their mother is in prison, remember? We'll see what happens."

"Screw that," Brody waved his hand. "You let Uncle Brody and Auntie Kacie watch them. Bring them up to our house and we can swim and hang out the whole week."

"Yeah, cause that's what you need at your house," I teased, throwing a pen across the room at him. "More kids."

Chapter 5

BRODY

DECEMBER WAS WHIPPING BY FASTER than I wanted it to. Not only was our hockey schedule crazy, we were playing well. Like . . . really, really well, which only made Coach Collins want to practice more. In fact, we'd never had a better start to a season than we had the last two months. The locker room was buzzing with reporters, press conferences were taking longer, and we were being asked to do more signing engagements. While all of that was awesome and a total blessing, I still had a bunch of stuff going on at home too.

When I wasn't at the rink, I was doing what I could to help Kacie with her idea of the perfect Christmas. We were baking cookies, taking the girls to lunch with Santa, and wrapping dozens of presents once they finally fell asleep. Add to that, secretly plotting with all of our friends behind Kacie's back to make sure every piece of my surprise puzzle fit together just right, and I was exhausted. Keeping secrets from your super inquisitive wife was a full-time job. But . . . we were almost there. We were only a few days away from the big reveal, and I could not *wait* to see the look on her face when she stepped into the family room at Sophia's and saw that it was full of her friends. The only thing that excited me more was getting to tell her that they were all staying for the next week, including Christmas day.

My phone rang from my back pocket and I pulled it out, smiling to myself when Kacie's cute face filled the screen. "Hey, hotness," I answered.

"Hi." She let out a heavy, dramatic sigh.

"What's wrong?" I laughed. "You sound tired."

"I *feel* tired."

"What did you guys end up doing yesterday?" I asked as I hung my duffel bag on the metal hook inside the Blackhawks locker room. Kacie had been spending every free minute over at her mom's house the last few weeks trying to get everything ready for her big move.

"I sanded and stained an old dresser that mom had in storage, helped Fred put a small fence up around the garden to keep the animals out, and painted half of the kitchen cabinets."

I set the phone down and quickly pulled my t-shirt over my head. "You did all that yesterday?" I asked when I picked it back up.

"Yep. And there's still *so* much more to do today."

"Well, I can't wait to see it . . . and I can't wait to see *you*."

"I can't wait to see you too. Sometimes I kinda wish you had the type of job where you could call in sick and play hooky for a day or two."

I let out another quick laugh. "You'd rather I be a plumber or something?"

"A plumber could be fun." Her voice lowered, "Imagine all the fun games we could play. I could be the lonely housewife and you could be the hot, strapping young plumber who comes to the house to rod my pipes . . ."

"Kacie—"

"It could be really, really *wet* under my sink and you'd have to climb under there and see what's causing all that wetness . . ."

"Seriously—"

"And while you're laying on your back, I would stand over the top of you, hike my robe up and—"

"Kacie!" I interrupted. "Holy shit. I'm about to go out on the ice for practice and now my dick is hard."

"Sorry," she apologized unconvincingly with a giggle.

"I'm pretty sure you're not."

"You're right. I'm not. I'm tired and horny and I want you here," she pouted. As bad as I felt that she was so stressed and worn out it was playing perfectly into my plan, and I could barely contain my smile.

I cleared my throat to pull myself together. "So here's what I'm thinking . . . I get home late Friday night, right?"

"Yeah," she said sadly.

"Well, we have an off day on Saturday. Let's get up early, take the girls to your mom's and spend the whole day together. We can go out to lunch, finish grabbing the last-minute stocking stuff for the girls, and maybe sneak in a quickie in the backseat of the car at the mall?"

Her soft but hearty laugh filled my ear. "Always the romantic, aren't you?"

"Okay, fine. We can skip lunch."

"You're adorable . . . and that sounds like a lot of fun. Let me talk to mom and get back to you, though. I have to make sure she doesn't already have plans."

"I already talked to her."

"You did?" her voice rose in surprise.

Not exactly, but she knows I have to get you out of the house on Saturday, so this works.

"Yep," I fibbed proudly.

"Brody Michael Murphy, you're the cutest."

"Is that a yes?"

"It's a date."

I sent Sophia a quick text to let her know the plan, and the countdown to Kacie's surprise officially began.

The girls were just getting into bed as I got home Friday night. I read Emma a few books, rocked Grace until her head fell heavy against my chest, and stopped by Lucy and Piper's room once I heard Kacie turn the shower on in the master bathroom.

I closed the door quietly behind me and sat on the end of Piper's bed. "How's it going?"

"Good." Piper gave me a huge grin with her mother's sparkling, excited eyes.

"Did you guys help Gigi a little bit today?" I looked from her to Lucy.

"Yeah. We couldn't do as much as we wanted because mom called Gigi and said she was picking us up to take us to the library for story time with Santa." Lucy shrugged.

I pressed my lips together and took a long, deep breath. I'd be lying if I said I wasn't just a little nervous about everything coming together like I was hoping it would. "Okay, well, if all the decorating isn't done it's not really the end of the world. It's more important that everyone gets here on time and that your mom is totally surprised."

Big smiles broke out across both of their faces.

"You guys remember to be a big help to Gigi tomorrow, okay? Whatever she needs . . . decorating, watching Grace, anything. Okay?"

They both nodded.

I stood up and walked over to each of the girls, kissing the tops of their heads before they curled down into their beds. "Alright, get some sleep, Twinkadinks. Big day tomorrow."

The next morning, I was up way before my alarm, staring at the clock like a little kid on Christmas morning. I had just started to drift back to sleep when my phone lit up. I glanced over my shoulder to make sure Kacie was still sleeping and picked it up on my way to the bathroom. It was a text from Sophia.

> **Sophia:** Hey. Fred and I made a big pot of coffee last night and stayed up decorating together. Any chance you can somehow get her to let you bring the girls over today? We don't want her seeing the stuff early.

My eyes darted around the bathroom as I wracked my brain, trying to think of a way to get Kacie let me take the girls over to Sophia's.

> I'm sure I can think of something. Eleven o'clock still work?

> **Sophia:** Yep, totally fine. What time did you say you told everyone to be here?

> No later than six. She wanted to watch A Christmas Story with the girls tonight so I'm not sure I can keep her out past seven.

> **Sophia:** Got it! See you in a while.

I quietly opened the door to sneak back to bed and came face to face with a blinking, sleepy Kacie. "Hey," she said as she rubbed her eyes. Noticing my phone in my hand, she pulled her brows in tight and looked up at me. "What are you doing?"

I shrugged. "I was checking the weather. What do you think about going to the outdoor mall over in North Branch today?"

Her face lifted. "Oooh, we haven't been there in a while. Good plan."

Thank God.

She lifted her hand and covered her mouth as she let out a big yawn. "What time is it anyway?"

I glanced down at my phone. "Almost six."

"The girls won't be up for another hour yet, let's go back to bed."

"Now you're talking," I wiggled my eyebrows up and down.

She rolled her eyes. "No way. I'm still sore from last night."

"Sore? Really?"

She gave me a small, shy grin and nodded.

I puffed my chest out and strutted as I followed her back to the bed. "Well, that'll teach you to underestimate the hot neighborhood plumber and his magical pipe wrench, huh?"

A couple hours later, the house was chaos as usual and everyone was rushing around.

"Okay," Kacie ran her hand through her hair, "I know I showered last night, but I'm gonna go take another quick one. When I get out, I'll run the girls over to mom's while *you* shower. Deal?"

"Uh . . . sounds good." I smiled, trying not to let the panic show. I listened to her footsteps as they climbed the stairs, moved down the hall and into the bathroom. The pipes hummed as she turned the shower on, and as soon as I knew I was clear, I sprinted as quietly as I could up the steps.

I flung open Lucy and Piper's door, accidentally scaring the crap out of them before I started rambling. "Girls, hurry! Mom's in the shower, then she wants to take you to Gigi's, but Gigi texted me and said she and Fred decorated so we have to get you over there before mom gets out!"

Their eyes grew huge as they jumped off their beds and started running in circles.

"Lucy," I called out, pointing at her, "Can you make sure that Emma has actual clothes on and not just a cape and Peppa Pig underwear?"

"I'll do my best," she said as she rushed out of the room.

"And you—" I turned to Piper, "—I'm gonna pack a bag for Grace real quick. Can you put her coat on her and bring her downstairs."

"Got it," she agreed. I followed her down the hall to Grace's room and grabbed the backpack from the closet. In one motion, I pulled her dresser drawer open and started throwing clothes in the bag haphazardly. There was a good chance it was nothing but shorts and tank tops, but I didn't have time to care. I grabbed a handful of diapers, stuffed those into the bag, zipped it shut and ran down the stairs. Piper stood by the front door holding Grace, just like I'd asked her to do, and a minute later, Lucy came down with Emma. I opened the door and shuffled them out to the car quietly.

Ten minutes later, I was back home and out of breath. I inhaled slowly through my nose and tried to slow my breathing as Kacie came down the stairs with a towel wrapped around her hair. She frowned as her eyes moved left to right around the kitchen. "Uh . . . where is everyone?"

"Surprise!" I held my arms out wide. "I packed their bags and took them to your mom's already."

Her mouth dropped open. "What? Why? I didn't even get to say good-bye."

"I was just trying to save us some time. We're only gonna be gone for a few hours, babe." I put my hands on her shoulders and turned her around, walking back toward the stairs. "Hurry. Go get ready so we can come home and watch our movie together tonight."

"Okay." She sounded kinda mopey but I knew just how to cheer her up.

"Hey—" I smacked her ass as I followed her up the stairs, "—on a scale from one to ten, how firm was that no about the quickie in the mall parking lot? The plumber has another tool he'd like to show you."

Chapter 6

Kacie

"I CANNOT BELIEVE YOU DID this," I shook my head slowly before laying it on Brody's shoulder. He lifted his arm and put it around me, pulling me tight against him.

"I'm pretty amazing, aren't I?"

"You are," I agreed.

I thought we were going to shop like Brody said, but after lunch at an adorable little cafe right on the river, we stepped outside and I was surprised to see a horse drawn carriage waiting for us. As Brody held my hand, I stepped up into the black carriage and the driver handed each of us a tall Styrofoam mug of steaming hot chocolate. We sat back against the private carriage seat and away we went.

"Do we have to go home?" I joked with a happy sigh. We were only halfway or so into our ride, but the simplicity of being in that carriage cuddled up under a blanket with Brody, breathing in the chilly air as we rode around the small downtown area, was the perfect break that I needed. Life had been so crazy lately, between hockey and mom's house and everything else, that I'd started to forget the simple things . . . like how amazing my sexy husband smelled, and how good his arms felt around me.

"We don't have to go home, but you're the one who has to call your mom and tell her she's the proud new mother of four crazy girls." He chuckled and his chest vibrated against my head.

"Are you kidding me? She'd probably love that. We're really so lucky to have her, you know that?"

He nodded. "We are."

My eyes dropped to the burgundy lipstick mark on my hot chocolate cup. "I think that's why this thing has been so hard for me."

Brody looked down at me, "What do you mean?"

"The inn is special to me, obviously, and I'm super sad to see it go, but I'm mostly sad to see mom go. I love having her right next door."

"Awww, honey." He pressed his lips against my temple and kissed me, lingering there for just a second. "I know you do, but she's only going five minutes away. You'll still see her all the time. And . . . now that she doesn't have to be doing stuff around the inn all the time, you'll probably see her even more."

"Yeah, I didn't think about that part."

"And you have to know that all you're doing over there to help means the world to her."

"I know it does," I nodded. "And I'm happy to do it. As much as I don't want to admit it, the place is kinda cute. It's old and definitely needed a lot of work, and will still need a lot even after they're in, but it's perfect for them. And they're so happy. I've never seen my mom smile more."

I sniffed. It was part the cold air and part feeling emotional about my mom and all the changes that were happening in my life.

He reached down and wrapped his big, warm hand around mine, squeezing it. "Did this whole inn thing ruin your perfect

Christmas?"

My face snapped up to his, "Ruin it? No. Change it? Maybe a little." I shrugged. On the upside, I learned how to tile a kitchen backsplash, so that's something." I gave him a huge, cheesy grin.

A sexy smirk crossed his lips, "Good. Now we have a plumber *and* a tile person in the family."

After the carriage ride, we shopped until our feet ached and we felt like we couldn't take one more step. The drive home was about half an hour, but as soon as Brody turned onto the highway, I fell sound asleep.

"Hey, beautiful. We're home," Brody said softly as he brushed my cheek with the back of his finger.

I cracked my eyes open and my house slowly came into focus. I sat up and tilted my head side to side, rubbing my sore neck. "I'm so tired. Wanna do the movie with the girls another night?"

"Fine with me," he shrugged.

"Good." I opened the car door and stood, stretching my arms high above my head. "Do you mind getting them from mom's for me? I'm gonna go in and take these shoes off."

"Uh . . ." he stammered nervously, staring at me with panic on his face, "Why don't you come with me? I'm sure the girls are excited to see you."

I frowned and dropped my arms. "I'm excited to see them, too, but can't I see them in ten minutes when you bring them home?"

He nodded his head toward the path through the woods that led to mom's. "Come on. Walk with me. I wanna hold your hand." He shot me his signature boyish grin.

"Ugh," I playfully mumbled under my breath. "That smile . . . kryptonite."

The pebbles crunched under our feet as we made the short trek to my mom's house in silence. We climbed the wooden steps of the porch and I froze, staring at the door.

"Look," I pointed. "She put her wreath up."

"Maybe she decided to do a few small things after all," he responded nonchalantly.

"I hope she put her tree up too. The girls would love that so much!" I reached out and turned the doorknob. As soon as the door swung open, I heard my mom hush someone loudly from the kitchen. I turned back to Brody and pulled my brows down low. "Did you hear that? I wonder who's here?"

I closed the door and walked around the corner toward the back of the house. Just as I crossed through the doorway into the great room, my heart soared into my throat.

"Surprise!"

Viper and Michelle with Matthew, Maura, and Michael.

Andy and Dani with Becca and Logan.

Derek and Alexa and their daughter, Hayley.

Tommy and Lauren, and their sons, Max and Alex.

Fred, mom and the girls.

All of my favorite people in the whole world were standing together in one room, huddled together against the far wall . . . smiling at me.

Silently, I stood with my hands over my mouth, trying to figure out what the hell was going on. I looked from them to Brody to my mom and back again. "What . . . I don't even . . . what's happening?" I finally asked.

"Well—" mom said slowly as she walked toward me and wrapped her arm around my shoulder, turning to face my friends. She motioned toward Brody, "—this amazing husband of yours felt so bad when you were upset about me selling the inn, that he rounded up all of your friends and asked them to come and stay here for the next week."

My mouth dropped open as I gasped softly. "Here? For a whole week?" I looked over at Brody, who was smiling as big as I'd ever seen him. "You did this? For me?"

He shoved his hands in his jean pockets and nodded, his

cheeks turning pink.

"Can we go play now?" Piper asked, but before the question was out of her mouth, all of the kids scampered off down the hall toward the playroom.

"I don't even know what to say. I can't believe this." I walked over and wrapped my arms around Brody's waist, laying my head against his chest as my eyes flooded with happy tears.

"My turn!" Alexa sniffed as she and Lauren came across the room with wide-open arms. I hugged my friend so hard I thought I might break every single one of her ribs, but I refused to loosen my grip. I held one arm out, inviting Lauren into our hug, and she gladly accepted, locking her arms around both of us at the same time. We swayed back and forth, elated to be together and crying on each other's shoulders. The three of us hadn't been together in several months. Kids, schedules, and life just seemed to keep getting in the way.

"I'm so glad you guys are here." I finally let go and wiped my eyes on the sleeve of my jacket.

Alexa stepped over to the island and grabbed the tissue box, offering it to me and Lauren. "We're glad too. When Brody called last month, it was a no-brainer."

"Last month?" I exclaimed.

She nodded. "He's been planning this for a really long time. But . . . Lauren and I can only stay tonight, not the whole week. We already had family plans so we both have to leave in the morning."

"That's okay," I shook my head and squeezed both of their hands. "I'll take you for as long as I can have you."

Lauren giggled as she cleaned the mascara from under her eyes. "Though, I'm pretty sure when Brody called and asked us to hang here for a week, Tommy was more than willing to blow off Christmas at his parents."

Our eyes all moved to Tommy, the world's biggest Wild fan, who was standing in between Brody and Viper with wide, awe-struck eyes.

"Look at him. He's pathetic," Lauren shook her head. "Babe! Your hockey boner is showing again."

Tommy turned back and gave her a huge grin, but denied nothing.

"Speaking of hockey," Brody stepped over. "We should probably talk about that."

"Okay?" I answered nervously.

"We still have games early next week, so tomorrow night me and Viper are heading back out of town, and Andy's coming along too," he said.

Tommy opened his mouth to talk, but Lauren held a finger up against his lips.

"Before you say a word, no . . . you aren't going with them," she said.

Like a scolded toddler, he closed his mouth and pouted.

"The *good* news is, that while the boys are gone, we're going to have the coolest girls sleepover ever," Michelle added with an excited grin as she walked over and tucked her arm inside of Viper's.

"Awwww, that's so fun," I said, a million ideas of what we could do racing through my head. I turned back to Brody. "And you guys will be home when?"

"The night before Christmas Eve . . . late," he answered.

I turned back to my group of friends. "You guys, I'm just so excited about this. I'm so excited that you're all here at the inn for one last week." A knot formed in my throat and I struggled to swallow it. "I'm sure Brody explained that mom was selling and I'm obviously really sad about it, but having you all here for the week makes the last Christmas at the Cranberry Inn so incredibly special and I am so thankful for all of you." I shifted my eyes over to Brody. "I'm especially thankful for *you*."

I walked over and raised up on my tippy toes, planting a kiss right on Brody's lips, not caring who watched us.

"Would you two knock that off," Viper teased, throwing a

pillow from the couch at us. "Knowing you two, you'll end up pregnant again."

I pulled back and licked my lips, my eyes focused on Brody's. We were thinking the same thing, but only we knew it. He narrowed his eyes at me and I gave him a small nod.

"Funny you should mention that, Lawrence!" Brody boasted as he turned toward Viper and puffed his chest out.

Viper's eyes darted from him to me. "No way!" he said with a stunned look on his face.

"Yes way, young Finkle. It appears that a little before Halloween time, Kacie and I made another little pumpkin of our own."

"Oh my God!" Michelle called out as several gasps came from our group of friends.

All at once, the room was a flurry of hugs and handshakes and congratulations. Brody and I hadn't yet discussed how, or when, we were going to tell everyone, but the moment came along and we went with it.

"So . . . is it too early to start taking bets on this baby being a girl too?" Viper teased, wrapping his arms around Brody and squeezing hard as he lifted him off the ground.

"Wait!" Dani called out. "Do you guys already know what you're having?"

"No," I shook my head. "I've had one doctor appointment but that's it. I'm just ten weeks."

"Another girl would be fine with me," Brody said. "I teased Kacie once that we were going to keep trying till we had a boy, but I've grown kinda fond of the Murphy girls. I wouldn't mind another one."

As a collective sigh came from the women in the room, I looked around for my mom. She was standing in the kitchen with Fred, wiping her eyes with a tissue.

I hurried over to her. "Are you upset with me? I'm sorry I didn't tell you sooner, or more privately. It just kinda happened."

Her emerald green eyes bore into mine and she shook her head vigorously. "Oh, honey! No! I'm not upset with you, not at all. I'm just . . . I don't know what I am." She paused and swallowed hard. "I'm worried that because we're moving I won't be as close to this baby as I am the others."

"Aw, mom—" I pulled her into a tight hug, "—yes, you will. I'll make sure of it. Anytime you want to snuggle with this little nugget, you just call and we'll drive him or her over for a sleepover at Gigis' house."

"Deal," she sniffed with a smile as she let go.

"The house looks amazing, by the way. I can't believe you did all this just for us."

"Yeah, well, I had a cute little elf who was a really big help." She turned her head and shot Fred a quick glance.

"Hey, Kacie!" Viper called out, pulling my attention from my mom to him.

"Yeah?"

"I need a plumber. Do you by any chance have a good recommendation for me?" he asked with a straight face as Brody was doubled over, laughing hysterically behind him.

Chapter 7

BRODY

VIPER, ANDY, DEREK, TOMMY, AND I stayed up way later than we should have and drank way more beers than we should have.

"Collins is going to kick our asses at practice tomorrow," I said to Viper, lifting my beer in the air.

"Correction. He's going to kill *you*. I don't drink, remember?" he rebutted.

"Why don't you drink, anyway?" Andy asked, popping the cap off another beer.

Viper shrugged. "I don't know. It's just never really been my thing."

"I was surprised when I found that out," Derek said.

"Most people are," Viper shrugged. "They assume because I'm a hockey player and all tatted up that I must be a big partier, too, but that part is totally wrong. I'm a lover, not a drinker."

"I believe the saying is 'I'm a lover, not a fighter.'" I laughed.

"I know, but I'm definitely a fighter so I had to improvise."

He wiggled his eyebrows up and down.

"So let's talk about hockey . . ." Tommy said, lifting his eyes from the table to Viper and me. "You guys are good this year. Like, really good. Think it might be Minnesota's turn to *finally* bring the Stanley Cup home?"

The Minnesota Wild had never won the Stanley Cup in franchise history, and with the way we'd been playing, people were starting to get excited. That excitement also came with a lot of nervous pressure.

"I don't know." I took a long, deep breath, puffing my cheeks out when I let it go. "I'm not gonna lie and say it hasn't crossed our minds, but we don't talk about it because all of us are crazy superstitious."

"Really?" Derek's voice rose in surprise. "Superstitious?"

I nodded. "Oh yeah. You wouldn't believe the weird shit that goes on in our locker room."

"Like what?" he asked.

"Well, that crazy bastard right there—" I pointed at Viper, "—has to put all of his left pads on before his right ones. He also has to be the last on and the last off the ice for every single game."

"I noticed that one . . . the ice one," Tommy said.

"And Mr. Golden Goalie over there has to drink one of those small bottles of orange juice before every home game," Viper teased.

Derek and Tommy turned toward me in unison.

"Only the home games?" Derek asked.

Viper answered before I could. "He switches to apple juice for the away games."

"Why?" Tommy asked.

I gave him a quick shrug. "There was this one really important game back in college. My coach at the time told me that word had gotten out about me and the stands were gonna be packed with scouts and agents. I was a ball of fucking nerves.

Someone asked if I wanted something to drink to help calm me down and I said sure." I grabbed a peanut from the bowl on the table and cracked it open. "They brought me orange juice. I didn't even think about it, I just drank it. It made me even crazier. Not only did I have a shut out that night, I had a few really amazing saves and, ever since then, I have orange juice before every game."

Derek cocked his head to the side and frowned, "But not away games."

"Not anymore," I shook my head. "I used to do it for away games, too, but I played like total shit once, so I switched it up. So far it's working for me."

"Wow," Tommy said incredulously, leaning back in his chair and folding his arms across his chest. "I had no idea hockey players could be that superstitious."

"I think a lot of athletes do crazy shit like this, but to us . . . it's normal." I laughed. "Well, as normal as we can get."

"I, for one, am hoping like hell that you guys go all the way," Andy, who'd been pretty quiet most of the evening, finally said. "Not only selfishly, because it would look great on my résumé, but for you two . . . and your whole team. You guys deserve it."

"I'll drink to that." I lifted my beer bottle in the air briefly and took a long drink. The other guys followed suit.

"What are you guys raising your glasses to?" Kacie called out from the family room. I looked over at her and she arched an eyebrow, smirking at me.

"We're toasting how incredible we all are for putting up with your asses," I teased back.

"Psh—" Michelle rolled her eyes, "—I'm pretty sure that's the other way around."

"Wow," I said softly, turning back to Viper. "Your woman answered that pretty quickly, dude."

He pulled the corner of his mouth up and gave me a quick

nod. "She's totally right, though. I'm definitely the pain in the ass of the two of us."

"Why don't all of you pain in the asses come sit with us?" Alexa slurred, waving us over with one hand as she almost knocked her wine glass out of her other hand.

"Whoa," I mumbled, looking at Derek.

"I know." He pressed his lips together, closed his eyes and nodded. "It's going to be a long road trip tomorrow. I'm gonna need barf bags for sure."

Just then, there was a soft knock on the front door. Kacie sat up straight and frowned at me as I glanced down and checked the time on my phone.

10:53

Perfect!

"Who's that?" Kacie asked, climbing to her feet.

As she walked toward me, I gave her an innocent shrug. "How am I supposed to know?"

She pursed her lips together and rolled her eyes dramatically. "You know everything."

"That's true," I agreed playfully.

I followed along behind Kacie as she made her way up to the front. She pulled the wooden door open and squealed so loudly I was sure dogs for miles around ran and hid under beds. She thrust her water bottle against my chest, knocking the cap off and spilling it all over my shirt in the process. Darla took a huge step forward and they crashed into each other, hugging and rocking back and forth.

"I didn't know you were coming too!" Kacie said through tears, her head resting against Darla's shoulder.

"Are you kidding? I wouldn't miss this for the world." Darla shot me a quick wink over Kacie's shoulder. "I wanted to get here earlier, but I had to finish my shift at the hospital before I could drive up."

Kacie peeked around Darla. "Did Neil come with you?"

"Uh," Darla said through a heavy sigh. "We'll have to talk about him . . . after a glass—or five—of wine."

"Uh oh." Kacie sucked in air through clenched teeth. "Well, come on in and tell us all about it."

It took a solid five minutes for Darla to make her way around the room, hugging and greeting her friends. I watched Kacie's sparkling eyes as they danced from person to person in the room, a huge smile plastered to her face.

That look . . . that smile . . . *that* was the reason I did everything I did. To watch the love of my life be that happy over something as simple as having all of her friends together in one room was worth every text, every headache, every stressful moment hoping it would all come together in the end.

Once Darla was in, we all crowded in the family room together. There wasn't an inch of free space on the couches and some people were sitting on the floor, but we didn't care. We just wanted to be together.

"Where are the kids?" Darla asked, taking a sip of her wine.

"In bed," Kacie said. "It's after eleven. They're all asleep in the playroom together like a bunch of mice, laying across each other."

Michelle shook her head. "No, your mom went in a little bit ago and straightened everyone out, covered them up and turned the TV off."

"Of course she did." Kacie rolled her eyes with a giggle. "Okay, so tell us why Neil isn't with you."

Darla had gotten engaged to Neil awhile back and, shortly after, they both applied for jobs at Loyola and moved to Chicago. Considering he didn't come up with her, I'm assuming things weren't going well after all, if they were even still going.

Darla took a deep, heavy breath. "Okay, so here goes. Apparently Neil, aka Doctor-Sparkling-Water, was really Doctor-Couldn't-Keep-His-Dick-In-His-Pants."

The girls all gasped as I looked over at Viper, whose jaw started ticking. Darla and Viper obviously had a history, but they would always be good friends. I knew he wanted to kill any guy that messed with her, especially Neil. He hated that guy.

Hated. That. Guy.

"I found out that he was sleeping with half the nurses in the NICU." She took a huge swig of wine, practically emptying her glass.

"How did you find out?" Kacie asked.

"Two nurses got into a screaming match in the hallway and I, along with a couple of other people, went over to break them up. In the chaos of it all, someone asked what they were screaming about and Sharon, the disgustingly skinny one, said she found out that Kandi was sleeping with Neil."

Kacie leaned forward on the couch, completely engrossed in Darla's story just like the rest of us.

"So anyway," Darla continued. "When I heard what she said, suddenly it became a three-way screaming match and let's just say I had the loudest voice. It was ugly, but in the end, it was him I should have been mad at . . . not them."

"Holy crap," Alexa said, hugging her wine glass.

"So . . . that was a couple of months ago. We broke up, he asked for the ring back, I told him to go fuck himself and then I sold it and bought myself a really nice TV."

"Atta girl," Viper said proudly.

She gave him a quick, tight smile and kept going. "I spent a few weeks feeling sorry for myself, but then I perked up and realized I had found my dream job in an amazing city and I had a lot to be thankful for, so screw him. One night, I went out with some friends and had one too many beers. I came home, decided I was going to die if I didn't have pizza rolls, so I turned the oven on, put them in, and then proceeded to pass out on the couch. An hour later, I woke up to the smoke alarm screeching, the kitchen all hazy, and the fire department banging on my door. Now, I'm dating Shane."

We all sat staring at her with deadpan expressions on our faces. I shook my head quickly. "Does anyone else feel like you somehow missed a huge part of the story?"

"Sorry." Darla giggled. "Shane is a fireman. My little Irish Chicago fireman who's hot and sweet and hot and wonderful . . ."

"But is he hot?" Kacie teased.

Darla raised her hand, pinching her fingers together. "Just a tad."

"Wait. Where is Mr. Hot and Wonderful?" Dani asked.

Darla tilted her head back and forth, staring up at the ceiling as she thought for a second. "I told him about it and we discussed it, but ultimately decided for him to stay back. We *really* like each other, so we're making an effort not to move too fast and ruin everything. I'll bring him up next time, for sure."

"Well." Michelle let out an exasperated sigh. "That's one hell of a story. Hopefully I remember it in the morning." She giggled as she tipped her wine glass back, swallowing what was left of it.

Without moving my head, I slid my eyes over to Viper, who watched Michelle lick the edge of her wine glass. He finally looked over at me and wiggled his eyebrows up and down. He raised his hand, cupping his mouth as he leaned toward me. "When she starts licking wine glasses, that's a good sign that the Viking is going to get to come out and blow his horn tonight."

I started coughing and choked on the gulp of beer I'd just drank. Wiping my lips with the back of my hand, I shook my head. "You have a way with words, Finkle. That's for sure."

Chapter 8

Kacie

THE NEXT MORNING I GOT up extra early, jumped in the shower and high-tailed it over to mom's, hoping to get breakfast going before everyone else woke up.

Just as I suspected, mom was already wide-awake and had every single burner on the stove cooking something different.

"What are you doing?" I asked quietly as I walked over and put my arm around her, kissing her cheek gently.

"You know me. I can't ever sleep, so I figured I'd get up and get breakfast going. It's gonna take a while."

"I know. That's why I tried to get over here early. What can I do?" I turned the sink on and started sudsing up my hands.

"Uh . . ." She turned halfway and looked around the kitchen, the corner of her mouth pulled up as she thought about what she wanted me to do next. "Fruit! There are going to be a million hungry little monsters in here in a little while and they love fruit. Start cutting up all the fruit you can get your hands on."

"Got it." I went to the fridge and pulled out strawberries, blueberries, and raspberries, dropping them all together in the big colander on the counter.

"So last night was pretty fun, huh?" Mom put her hand on her hip and started flipping crackling pieces of bacon over in the pan.

"It was fun. I think I'm still in shock, actually. I can't believe Brody did all that."

"You know . . . he told Brody not to say anything, but this whole thing was Viper's idea."

I froze and spun toward her slowly. "*Viper?*"

She nodded without turning around. "Uh huh. I mean . . . Brody was wracking his brain, trying to think of a way to save your perfect Christmas, and Viper threw this out to him. Brody did all the calling and planning, but the idea started with Viper."

"Wow," I shook my head in amazement. "If you would've told me to guess who suggested this to Brody, Viper would have been my last guess."

"I know," she scoffed. "That boy has a lot more good in him than people realize."

"He does," I agreed with a nod as I plucked the stem off a strawberry. Viper and I got along great for the most part, but last year after an incident with Michelle, I kinda let him have it. Things have been a little tense ever since, but him suggesting all of this to Brody really meant a lot to me.

"Hey!" Mom called out with a laugh. "No time for breaks."

I jumped and swung my head toward her, not even realizing that I'd stopped cutting and zoned out. "Sorry," I shook my head quickly. "I was just thinking about Viper and got a little lost."

"Oooh, you were thinking about me?" A familiar voice quipped from the doorway of the kitchen. I turned my head and Viper, wearing black pajama pants with big Santa heads on them, grinned at me.

I rolled my eyes. "Don't let it go to your head. I wasn't thinking of you like that. Mom was just telling me that this weeklong party thing started out as your idea and then Brody ran with it." I walked over and planted a soft kiss on his cheek. "So thank you. It means a lot to me that you cared too."

"Anything to help my boy get laid," he joked. I pulled my hand back and smacked him hard in the stomach. "I'm kidding, I'm kidding," he said through a laugh. "First of all, obviously homeboy gets laid plenty, the evidence of that being the newest little bun in your oven. And B, I really *do* care." He put his arm around my shoulders and pulled me toward him, kissing me above the temple.

"Get your lips off my wife before I remove them from your body." Brody barked playfully as he came through the back door.

"Awww, come here, Brody. I have a kiss for you too. Don't worry." Viper held his arms out straight in front of him and strode across the room toward Brody, who laughed and slapped him away.

"All these people in here and I'm the only one working," mom said as she shot us a wink.

"Sorry!" I apologized again, returning to the strawberries.

"Good morning, babe." Brody nuzzled into my neck. "I didn't even hear you get up this morning. How early did you sneak out?"

I shrugged. "A while ago. I didn't want to wake you."

"What can I help with, Sophia?" Viper clapped his hands loudly, rubbing them together.

"Uh—" mom craned her neck and peeked over at the pan of cinnamon rolls on the counter, "—those rolls should be cool enough by now. Would you mind icing them?"

"You got it," he said.

"Good morning!" Lauren sang happily as she came into the kitchen.

"Ugh, isn't she the *most* annoying human first thing in the morning?" Alexa grumbled from right behind her.

One by one, people started flowing into the kitchen and everyone began fluttering around setting the tables, pouring milk and juice into cups, cutting eggs and sausage into super tiny pieces so they were ready for all the little ones. It was chaos, but wonderful chaos.

An hour later, the chaos was over and the kitchen looked like a tornado had gone right through the middle of it.

"Holy cow," I said in awe as I surveyed the damage.

"How can they make *that* much of a mess so quickly?" Michelle muttered.

"I'll tell you what," Brody declared. "Since Alexa and Lauren are leaving in a little while, and since we'll be out of town for the next couple days leaving all the kid stuff to you girls, the boys are going to clean the kitchen this morning."

"We are?!" Viper exclaimed.

"Yes, we are," Brody repeated, throwing a balled up napkin at his head.

Viper grimaced as he opened and closed his right hand. "I'm not sure I can. I think I strained something in my hand yesterday."

Andy stood and lightly slapped Viper in the back of the head. "You really should give that hand a rest once in a while. Now get up!"

Brody came over and took my hand, pulling me up from the chair. "I'm gonna turn the fireplace on while you girls get cozy in the family room. We'll take care of everything."

"Thanks." I gave him a quick kiss on the lips and headed toward the family room with the other girls right behind me. We all collapsed on different couches and talked the next hour away, while intermittently breaking up fights over Legos and changing a few diapers.

Just as the boys finished the kitchen, Alexa glanced over at Lauren and sighed. "It's about that time, Lauren."

Lauren's already pouty bottom lip stuck out dramatically. "I know. I was waiting for you to say it."

My heart sank. "This sucks."

"It totally sucks," Lauren agreed.

Michelle and Dani met Lauren and Alexa because of me, and didn't talk to them as much as I did, but they were clearly sad to see them go too. The day we'd all spent together went by way too fast, but was amazing none-the-less.

"Can we do this another time? Like . . . just for fun?" Lauren sniffed as she stood.

My heart sank even lower. "That would be awesome, but where? The inn won't be mom's for much longer."

"You could always twist my arm and drag me away for a spa weekend," Alexa said with a laugh.

Michelle sprang up from the couch and pointed at Alexa, "Yes! That sounds like fun. Let's do that. Kids and husbands stay home and we spend a couple of days—or a couple of months—at the spa."

"A couple of months?" Viper rolled his eyes as he stepped into the family room and wrapped his arms around Michelle's waist from behind, resting his chin on her shoulder. "You can barely go a couple of hours without the Viking, let alone a couple of months."

She giggled and gave him a hard elbow, right in the stomach.

We helped Lauren and Alexa pack up their stuff and the kids and then said a tearful good-bye in the driveway. I don't think anyone was more disappointed than Tommy, who really *did* want to stay and hang . . . mostly with Brody and Viper.

After they pulled away and I shut the door, Brody pulled me against him, the sound of his heart thumping loudly against my ear. "Sorry they had to go so soon."

I took a long, slow breath. "I'm sorry too. There never seems to be enough time with them, but . . . this little bit was better than nothing."

"Good point. Hopefully you feel that way about me, too, because I need to start packing up so we can head to the airport in a few hours."

My shoulders slumped. I'd either forgotten, or totally blocked out, that he, Viper, and Andy would be leaving also. "Oh, yeah, that's right."

"Don't be bummed. We're playing two quick games and we'll be home before you know it. Then, it'll be time for the Christmas morning of all Christmas mornings. Can you even imagine how many presents are going to be in that room with all these kids here?"

"Santa's gonna need one hell of a sleigh," I joked as we walked hand-in-hand back toward the family room.

Chapter 9

BRODY

OUR PLANE LANDED IN NASHVILLE, but rather than head to the hotel with the rest of the team, we waited around for Andy's plane, which was about twenty minutes behind ours.

"Sucks that he couldn't get on the same flight as us," Viper grumbled as he shifted uncomfortably in the blue airport chair.

"It's only twenty minutes or so. Not that big of a deal."

"Yeah, but these chairs fucking suck."

I glanced over and watched him fidget and stretch, trying to find a comfortable spot. "Did you want me to get you a bottle, you big baby?"

"Shut up." He finally stopped moving and let out a heavy sigh.

"Did you get Michelle a Christmas present yet?" I asked, hoping I could distract him enough that he'd quit complaining about the seat.

His eyes lit up in a way that usually meant trouble. "Hell yeah I did. And I think she's gonna go nuts."

"What'd you get?"

"I had one of those mothers necklaces made for her. You know . . . the ones where the kids' birthstones are in there? She mentioned wanting one when we had Michael, but I never got around to it and I think she forgot. She's gonna freak out."

I nodded slowly. "Nice."

"Did you get Kacie anything yet?"

Turning toward him, I pressed my lips together and shook my head.

"What? Why not? You're screwed."

"I know. I've been thinking and thinking about it, but I just can't come up with anything. I mean . . . I can come up with a million things but none of them are special enough to go along with her *perfect* Christmas, ya know what I mean?"

"Yeah." He nodded as he stared straight ahead. "Need some suggestions?"

I crossed my arms over my chest as I sat back into the seat. "I'm kinda scared to ask, but go for it."

"Okay. There is always your typical fallback of jewelry, but then there are more . . . exotic options. How about, say, a stripper pole for your bedroom? Maybe some sexy Christmas lingerie that's red with white fur around the edge? Perhaps one of those sexy homemade coupon books? Ya know . . . present this coupon for one blow job?"

I frowned at him in horror, but said nothing. After a few seconds, he looked over at me. "What?" he asked defensively when he realized I was already staring at him.

"First of all, that coupon thing for a blow job? Yeah, that's a present for me, not for her. So is the lingerie and stripper pole. Stop giving me suggestions. I think you used all your smart brain cells on the Christmas party idea."

Viper let out a boisterous laugh and punched me in the arm. "Shut up, asshole. I have amazing ideas."

"Yeah, like one percent of the time," I teased. "The rest of the time, your ideas make Andy have to prepare a statement for the media."

"Oh God. I don't like hearing Andy, statement, and media in the same sentence," Andy said from behind us.

Viper and I both turned in our seats. "Hey! We thought you were coming from that way," I said as I pointed my thumb behind me.

"I was and then they switched my gate at the last minute. Now . . . do I even want to know what the hell you two are talking about?" His eyebrows lowered and he looked back and forth from me to Viper.

"This knucklehead was giving me gift ideas for Kacie and they weren't exactly . . . good." I rolled my eyes.

"Wait. You don't have a gift for Kacie yet?" Andy asked in a surprised tone.

"No. I don't," I defended. "Do you have Dani's present already?"

Andy nodded. "Yeah, I got it two months ago."

I stood up with a heavy sigh. "Let's go," I grumbled.

We got to the hotel and Viper had to pee, so he went straight to his room while I waited with Andy at the front desk.

"Why are you so damn grumpy tonight?" Andy asked after giving his license to the receptionist.

"I'm not grumpy. A little stressed, maybe, but not grumpy." I grabbed a mint from the bowl, unwrapped it and popped it into my mouth.

"Okay, then let me rephrase. Why are you so stressed?"

The receptionist handed him back his license and frowned down at the screen. "Unfortunately, Mr. Shaw, there's been a glitch in the system and I'm afraid we don't have a room available."

"What?!" Andy exclaimed.

She looked up at him; worry flooding her face. "I'm so, so sorry about that, but we've overbooked. I can give you a credit for a free stay in the future?"

He sighed in frustration and ran his hand through his hair. "What good is that going to do me tonight?"

The nervous receptionist shrugged and stared at him wide-eyed, like she was waiting for him to scream at her.

"Dude," I lightly smacked his chest to get his attention. "My room has two beds, why don't you just stay with me?"

Andy searched my face, hesitating for just a second. "Are you sure?"

"Totally. All that bed ever does is hold my suitcase, anyway."

"Thanks, bro." Andy turned toward the receptionist, "Alright, I'll just stay with him."

Her shoulders fell and I practically heard the air leave her lungs in relief. "Okay, I'm really sorry about that."

Andy gave her a quick wave before throwing the strap of his duffel bag over his shoulder. "Don't sweat it. Shit happens."

She shifted her eyes to mine and gave me a wide, thankful smile. I nodded quickly before Andy and I turned and headed toward the elevator.

We got to our room and dropped our bags on the floor next to the dresser.

"Why the hell is flying so exhausting?" Andy asked as he collapsed onto the bed. "All you're doing is sitting in a chair, exerting zero energy. So why when you land do you immediately feel like you need a nap?"

"Well, first of all . . . it's late so that nap would actually be called bedtime, and second, I have no idea about the other part." I sat on the edge of the other bed and lifted my hands, rubbing my tired eyes with the base of my palms.

"Okay, what's eating at you, dude? For real?"

I glanced over at Andy quickly before laying back on the bed and staring up at the dated popcorn ceiling of the hotel room. "I told you . . . I'm stressed."

"You're *this* worked up over a present for Kacie?"

"Andy . . . she's so awesome. She handles my career without skipping a beat and never complains about anything. She also never *asks* for anything. Low-maintenance is an understatement for her, which only makes me want to get her something that much more special. Jesus, the girl still clips coupons!"

He raised his head off the bed and frowned at me. "She does?"

"She does," I nodded and let out a laugh, thinking about my crazy wife. "And she wants the *perfect* Christmas . . . well, I need to give her the perfect gift to go along with it, but I'm coming up with nothing."

"I could ask Dani to hint around while we're here?" he offered.

"Nah. Thanks though. I'll come up with something . . . hopefully."

"Hopefully, when you do figure it out, we'll be home in time for you to actually give it to her."

I turned my head toward him. "What are you talking about?"

"My phone died on the plane, so I had nothing to do but listen to the two guys next to me go on and on about the storm moving through the Midwest in the next couple of days. I kinda blew it off, but then as I was getting off the plane, the flight attendants were talking to each other about it too." He raised his eyebrows, "Supposed to be a big one. Like . . . really big."

My stomach twisted into a huge knot. "That's not even funny."

Andy shook his head. "I'm not kidding."

I looked back up at the ceiling. "Well, those weather men better be wrong because the last thing in the entire fucking world I want to do is call my wife and tell her we won't make it home for Christmas."

"Alright, boys. Slight change in plans." Coach Collins let out a heavy sigh as he walked through the door of the locker room after our win over the Nashville Predators. He moved further into the room and lifted one foot onto the bench, resting his elbow on his knee as he rubbed his chin. I wanted him to stop talking. I knew what was coming was bad and I didn't want to hear it. "I just spoke with the front office and they've been watching the weather reports every minute tonight. There's a good-sized storm moving across the Midwest with strong wind gusts and they're not comfortable with us going up in the plane."

My eyes shot to Viper, whose own eyes grew wide as they slid over to me.

"They *have* agreed to let us take a bus since the roads still look pretty good at this point," he continued. "So get ready and head out there as quickly as you can. We're taking off ASAP to beat whatever weather we can."

It was rare that hockey games were ever canceled. Beyond rare, but with the way they were talking, this storm was going to be one of epic proportions.

The guys all started hustling around the locker room, throwing stuff in their bags and taking two-minute showers. No one said a word, but we didn't have to. We were all thinking the same thing and we knew it. Them canceling our flight was a big deal. Not making it to St. Louis for our next game would be a big, *big* deal so we were anxious to get on the road too.

"Shit!" I stood and froze, staring at Viper.

"What?" he asked but didn't look up from his locker.

"Andy."

"What about him?"

"What are we gonna do with him? He can't come on the bus with us."

"Ooooh," Viper said slowly, finally realizing what I was getting at. "Well, he's a grown man, Brody. He's gonna have to figure that shit out."

"I'll text him from the bus," I said with a sigh.

We boarded the bus quickly and were on the road within minutes. I pulled out my phone and sent Andy a text.

> Yo! As it turns out that storm really is a mess, so they put us on a bus to St. Louis instead of a plane. I feel bad that we left you behind but we didn't have a choice.

Staring out the window at the passing lights, I tapped my leg impatiently as I waited for his response. After a minute, my phone buzzed.

> **Andy:** Don't sweat it, man. I'm still gonna try and make my flight there and hope they don't ground it. I'll keep you posted.

I nodded to myself at his response and decided to text Kacie instead of calling her like I usually did. The last thing I needed was for my stress to make her stressed.

> Hey, babe! How's it going?

She responded almost immediately.

> **Kacie:** Hey! Good! We all sat around and watched you guys. Great game!

> Thanks! I felt good out there tonight. We all did.

> **Kacie:** It showed! So, the weather is all over the news up here. Have you heard anything about it at all?

I tried to downplay it as best as I could.

> Yeah, one of the guys mentioned something about it.

> **Kacie:** It looks bad, Brody. Really bad. They're talking feet of snow, not inches. Me, Michelle, and Dani ran to the store today and spent $500 to stock up on things for the next week. People were insane. And

we're used to snow up here, so that's saying a lot.

Fucking wonderful.

It's okay, babe. Don't freak out yet. These weather guys are wrong all the time, and sometimes things miss where they say they're going to hit.

Just as I sent that text to her, Viper turned his phone toward me. "Dude, look at this." The glow of his phone lit up his round, huge eyes. I squinted and studied his phone and within seconds, my eyes mirrored his. He'd pulled up the radar of the snowstorm and it was *huge.* It wasn't a wide storm, but it was long, stretching all the way from the top of Minnesota to the middle of Missouri and it looked like it was getting stronger as it moved across toward the Great Lakes. Before I could say anything, my phone buzzed again.

Kacie: I know, and I hope you're right. I'm just worried that if it does what they say it might do, you guys won't be able to make it home in time for Christmas. That would be a disaster!

Don't worry until it happens, okay, babe? How are my girls? What did you guys do today?

I changed the subject as smoothly as I could, but deep down I had the same worry Kacie did. As much as Viper and Andy felt like my brothers, and I loved them like family, I wanted to spend Christmas with my *real* family . . . Kacie and the girls.

Chapter 10

Kacie

I HARDLY SLEPT THAT NIGHT. THE TV in my room was turned low, but it stayed on the Weather Channel. I set my phone to get text alerts so that I didn't miss *any* breaking news. The storm was due to hit that day and I was a wreck. While I was happy that my mom, friends, and a bunch of kids were all cozied up at the inn together, I would finally be able to take a sigh of relief when Brody and the boys pulled into the driveway.

"Hey," Michelle said, coming through the kitchen doorway in her light blue robe.

My lips spread into a tight smile. "Good morning."

She froze and scowled at me. "That look. I don't like that look. What's wrong?"

"I'm just nervous about the weather." I ran my fingertip around the rim of my coffee mug, the steam warming my hand.

"Ugh," she groaned as she pulled the kitchen chair out and sat down across from me, resting her cheek against her hand. "I hear you. I watched the weather this morning and it made me sick. We're used to snow up here, so when people are freaking out and clearing the grocery store shelves, it's no joke."

"I know," I agreed. She was exactly right. Where we lived, snow was just a way of life. People in Minnesota knew how to prepare, how to move it quickly, and more importantly, when to panic. At the grocery store, it was obvious that panic had begun to set in. The guy behind the meat counter was asking every single person if they needed anything extra to ride out the storm. The bread shelf was almost empty, and there wasn't a water bottle or juice box in sight. Thankfully we got all we needed before it was cleared out, and if we ran short, mom's pantry was floor to ceiling mason jars filled with vegetables, jams, fruits and just about everything else you could imagine.

"Hi, Mama," Emma said from behind me.

I turned in my chair and scooped her up onto my lap, just like I did every morning. I gently pulled her head against my chest and we rocked back and forth. Emma was my wild child. My little spitfire who did her own thing and didn't care about anyone's approval. She was also my early-riser, which I didn't mind one bit. She spent most of the day running here or there and the mornings were the only time she moved slow enough for me to grab a few extra snuggles.

"Are all the other kids still sleeping?" I asked her.

She nodded and rubbed her eyes with balled up fists.

Originally, we'd planned on the kids sleeping in the guest rooms with their parents, but they were having so much fun all cuddled up in the playroom together that we decided to let them stay in there.

"Emma, what should we do today?" Michelle asked.

Emma looked over at her and shrugged. "Maybe build a snowman?"

Michelle's eyebrows went up. "That sounds fun!"

"We should build a daddy snowman, an Uncle Viper snowman, and an Uncle Andy snowman to surprise them when they get back," Emma added excitedly.

"Ooooh, now *that's* a good idea." I squeezed her thigh gently. "Hop down. I'm gonna make some breakfast and we'll get started."

As I opened the fridge, Dani walked into the kitchen, covering her yawn with the back of her hand. "Good morning, everybody."

"Morning!" I called out without turning around. I took a carton of eggs out of the fridge and started cracking them one by one into the pan.

"Can I help?" Emma asked as she walked up next to me.

"Of course," I said. I bent down and lifted her onto the counter. "Don't touch the metal part of the pan because it's hot, okay?"

She nodded.

Within minutes, hungry kids started filing into the kitchen so Emma and I started scrambling the eggs as fast as we could.

I scooped eggs onto a plate and passed it to Michelle, who added sausage and blueberries to each plate, and then handed it to Dani who set it in front of one of the kids.

"This is fun," Dani giggled. "Kind of like an assembly line or cafeteria or something."

I looked over at her with a smile. "Well, if you ever get sick of the whole glamorous sports agent thing, I think Lucy and Piper's school is looking for a new lunch server. You'd look pretty cute in a white apron full time."

"Serving lunch to a bunch of crazy, hormonal middle-school kids?" Darla exclaimed loudly as she walked into the kitchen. "I feel like *that* might truly be the toughest job on the planet."

I smiled at her. "Hey! I didn't hear you come down the stairs." You hungry?"

She pursed her lips together and crossed her arms over her chest. "Are you kidding? Look at me . . . I'm *always* hungry."

I rolled my eyes and a few of the kids giggled as they continued shoveling bites into their mouths.

"So, kids, what do you think about building snowmen this morning?" I asked as I made up four more plates and carried those to the island, setting them in front of Michelle, Dani, Darla, and an empty stool for me. "After breakfast, we're all gonna bundle up and go outside. Emma thought it would be fun to make snowmen that look just like your dads!"

Each of their little faces lit up and they all started yelling out ideas for the snowmen.

"For Brody's, we should put a baseball hat on it since he always wears a hat," Piper said.

"Yeah," Lucy blurted. "A Wild one."

"My daddy wears a suit," Becca said before turning to look at Dani. "Can we put a tie on our snowman?"

The corner of Dani's mouth pulled up and she looked at Becca sadly. "That's a great idea, Bec, but I have a feeling any ties he packed are with him on the road."

I covered my mouth with my hand as I talked through a big bite of eggs, "Brody has tons, you can use one of his."

"I think after breakfast, I'll let you guys run around and do that while I sleep for a little longer. I'm still pretty beat from working the other day then the long drive up here," Darla said.

"Okay," I said.

"This is going to be so much fun!" Piper exclaimed.

"I can't wait for them to see them when they get home!" Becca clapped excitedly.

Michelle, Dani, Darla, and I all shot each other the same worried glance, but didn't say a word.

Positive thoughts, positive thoughts, positive thoughts.

It took us almost an entire hour to get the kids all bundled up and out the door. By the time we were done, we were sweaty and so exhausted that we didn't even *feel* like going out, but we knew that if we let them wear themselves out for a while, we'd be rewarded with a nice, long, *quiet* nap time.

"Your mom is a saint, you know that?" Michelle said from behind me. I started to shovel a small path for us to follow through six inches of thick snow out into the yard, but she plucked the shovel from my hands and took over.

"Well, she's put up with me and all of my craziness for thirty years, so I do know that, but why do *you* think so?" I replied.

"She's in there watching Michael for me so I can be out here with you girls and the kids. She doesn't have to do that."

We got to the middle of the yard and the kids fell back and started making snow angels, blinking quickly as fresh flakes fell on their faces. Maura marched through the snow, lifting her little knees as high as she could until she found a comfortable place to plop her butt down, giggling wildly.

"Awww. I know she doesn't *have* to, but who are we kidding? She loves babies more than adults. Playing with him for a few days will tide her over until our little one gets here." I bent down and pulled Grace's hat further onto her head. She hated hats and I knew I'd be pulling it down five hundred times before we went back inside, but if it kept her little ears from getting frostbite, I didn't mind.

"Are you guys going to find out what you're having?" Dani asked.

"Probably," I said with a quick laugh. "Brody usually gets so excited when the ultrasound tech asks if we want to know, he blurts out yes before he even asks me."

"Does he really?" Dani asked incredulously, her dark eyes widening under the edge of her hot pink winter hat.

I nodded. "Yep, both times so far. And then on the way to the car, he high fives every single person we pass."

"He does not!" Dani blurted out.

"He sure does. This weird, euphoric, proud high takes over him and he has no control for a while." I took a few steps forward and fixed Grace's hat again. "Not gonna lie . . . it's adorable to watch."

"Can you imagine what's going to happen if this one is a boy?!" Michelle exclaimed.

"If we find out this one is a boy, it'll be a good thing my OB's office is right near the hospital because he'll probably have a heart attack." I bent down and picked up a wad of snow then packed it into a perfect ball in my hands. "Here, Lucy! Start a snowman with this." I tossed the ball to her.

"Do you have a feeling about it either way?" Michelle asked.

I shrugged, "Not really. I mean, I don't feel any different, but it's still pretty early."

"Wait." Dani looked back and forth from me to Michelle. "I don't get it. You *feel* different if it's a boy or a girl?"

"Some people think so, but I have no idea. I've only ever had girls." I answered.

Michelle chimed in, "I definitely carried my boys lower than Maura, but not until at least halfway through the pregnancy."

Dani took a deep breath, looking a little dazed as she stared off into the trees. "Wow."

I narrowed my eyes, searching her face. "Are you pregnant?"

Her head snapped over to me and she shook it quickly. "God, no!"

"Do you want to have more kids?" I asked.

She pinched her lips together and thought for a second about her answer. "Originally, I didn't think I wanted to have my own and Andy was fine with that, but when I see him playing in the backyard with Logan, or reading to Becca, or hear him laughing with them in the other room . . ." her voice cracked and she paused for a quick second, "In those moments, something twitches inside of me and I want to have one with him too. Maybe even twenty."

Michelle and I laughed out loud . . . hard. We both knew all too well the power of a man and a baby together and the impact it could have on blowing your ovaries to smithereens.

"Listen, let's pause this conversation and save it for later tonight because it sounds to me like it might be one of those longs ones—" I looked down at my feet and back up at them, "—and my toes are turning into little frozen sausages. Let's build these snow-husbands and go warm up by the fire."

"And keep an eye on that weather report," Michelle added in an uneasy tone. I specifically didn't look over at her because the worry that would be plastered all over her face would hop to my face and that would make my stomach start clenching all over again. I needed a break, and I needed to make a snowman.

"What now?" I asked the kids a few minutes later, as we all stood and stared at the three naked snowmen in the yard.

"Time to decorate!" Piper cheered.

"I'll go to our house and grab a few things to dress up our boys while you guys get sticks, rocks, and whatever else for their faces and arms, okay?" I said to Michelle, Dani, and the kids.

They nodded, and I started walking toward the small patch of trees that separated the inn from my house. Once inside, I made a quick pit stop in the bathroom, thanks to the little brussel sprout using my bladder as a trampoline, and then zipped around the house grabbing anything I thought would fit the boys' snowmen perfectly.

As I walked through the family room, I noticed the television had been left on. I carefully bent down and tried not to drop anything as I grabbed the remote to turn it off, but the sudden beeping coming from the screen caught my attention. Cliff Wilhelm, the local weatherman, appeared on the screen with a map of the Midwest behind him. Large portions of Iowa and Minnesota were covered in pink and he pointed at them as he talked about how many inches, or feet, of snow had already fallen in some places.

My stomach dropped. The boys were due back late the following night, but when Cliff said that several counties were under a blizzard watch already, I knew it wasn't looking good. The storm appeared to be getting stronger, not weaker. No way would they be able to fly into Minneapolis with that kind of snow. A lump the size of a walnut formed in my throat and it actually hurt to swallow. I finally cleared my throat and vowed to put a smile on my face as I walked back over to the inn. The snow might ruin *my* perfect Christmas, but no way would I let it ruin my daughters, too.

Chapter 11

BRODY

"ANYTHING CHANGED?" ANDY ASKED AS he walked out of the bathroom after his shower.

"Nope," I said with a sigh, staring at the weather report on the TV.

He sat on the edge of his bed and crossed his arms. "Well, we might want to start thinking about the inevitable."

"No," I said sternly. "That's not an option. We have to be home for Christmas."

"I get it, Brody. I do. I hate the thought of not being with my kids and Dani, too, but you know that I'm a realist and this doesn't look—"

"Just stop," I snapped as I stood quickly. "No flights have been canceled and no decisions have been made, so can we not go there yet." It was more of a statement than a question. "I'm taking a shower." I closed the bathroom door and leaned my back against it. I'd worked so hard for a month to pull everyone together and surprise Kacie with the perfect Christmas at the inn, no way could *I* not be there. I turned the shower on and welcomed the hot water that rolled over my skin, hopefully taking my shitty mood down the drain with it.

After I got out and dried myself off, I threw on my lucky sweats and Wild t-shirt and walked back out to the hotel room. Viper, who was sitting on the chair in the corner, stopped talking when he saw me. "Morning," I said to him with a nod.

He looked down at his phone and back up at me, "It's actually afternoon now."

I walked by Andy and gently smacked his shoulder. "Sorry about before."

"Don't mention it," he shook his head. "I know you're stressed. I am too."

"Lovers quarrel?" Viper teased.

I picked up a pillow off the bed and whipped it at his head. "No, asshole! We were talking about the weather and I got pissy."

"Eh, it'll be fine," Viper dismissed.

"I'm glad you're so confident. Wish I was." I plopped down on the bed and picked my phone up.

"I'm telling you, it'll work out. Leave it up to Viper Claus." He tapped his own chest arrogantly. "If I have to single handedly save Christmas—"

"Wait a minute, wait a minute, wait a minute . . ." I laughed. "Did you just say Viper Claus?"

His mouth curled into a wicked grin. "Ho, ho, ho motherfuckers!"

We stopped and grabbed a quick lunch together at a greasy spoon type of place on the way to the arena. I usually didn't like eating shitty food on game days, but my stomach had been in a knot for so long, I didn't think it mattered anymore.

"What can I get for you guys?" an older woman in a light blue polo, who looked and sounded like she'd worked there for at least thirty years, asked with a smile.

"Uh . . . what's good here?" I answered her question with a question.

"The fish and chips is excellent but we don't serve that until dinner, so I'd say a burger." She pointed down to the menu. "We have a bunch of different ones . . . one with avocado, one with barbecue sauce and a big onion ring, one with pulled pork on it. They're all fantastic."

My stomach growled as she listed off burger descriptions. "You had me at pulled pork. I'll take that one." I closed my menu and handed it to her.

Andy and Viper ordered the same and the waitress turned and went back to the kitchen.

"So, not to make your stress any worse, but have you given any more thought to what you're going to get Kacie? Or when the fuck you're even going to have time to go shopping?" Viper asked me.

I shrugged and looked down at the napkin under my glass. "I have a surprise for her, but it's not really a present. It seems kinda lame to give it to her for Christmas."

"Kacie's a sweet girl, Brody. She doesn't need jewelry and furs to make her happy. Shit, I doubt she'd even like that stuff," Andy said before he took a sip of his pop.

I shook my head. "She's totally not like that. She likes the little things, the sentimental stuff. Frankly, I doubt she even wants a gift, she just wants us home."

My phone beeped and a text from Kacie popped onto the screen.

"Her ears must have been ringing," I laughed, swiping at my phone.

Kacie: Hey, baby. Just checking in. How's it going?

Hey, honey. Good. The boys and I are just grabbing a bite to eat before we head over to the arena. How about you guys?

Kacie: We just came in from building snowmen out in the yard. We made hot chocolate and the kids are warming up by the fire. Hopefully after some lunch they're all going to crash.

Sounds like fun. Wish I were sitting by the fire with you guys.

Kacie: I wish you were here too. :(

Fuck you, sad face.

Don't be sad, baby. We leave right after the game tonight. I'll call you as soon as we board the plane.

Kacie: I've been watching the news non-stop, Brody. It looks terrible out there. Do you think the flight will be canceled?

I don't know. I'm trying not to worry about it until there's something to worry about.

Kacie: That's not exactly my thing. LOL!

I know . . . but try. Besides, Viper Claus has assured me that everything will be fine.

Kacie: Viper Claus?!

Don't ask. LOL! I'll call you, hopefully with good news, as soon as I know something, okay?

Kacie: Okay, babe. Love you.

Love you more!

"Kacie freaking out too?" Viper asked as I set my phone down.

"Yeah." I nodded toward his phone, "Did Michelle text you?"

"Yep, and Dani texted him," he tilted his head toward Andy. "It's like they synchronized their freakouts and texted us all at the same time."

Andy laughed and set his phone down. "I'm sure they'd be really happy you said that."

"I get it, though. I'm a little freaked out myself. I've never missed Christmas with my girls before. Frankly, the thought makes me sick." I let out a long, heavy sigh.

"Stop saying shit like that!" Viper roared. "We're not missing anything!"

Just then, the waitress walked up to the table carrying an arm full of plates and set one down in front of each of us. The tension at the table when she walked away wasn't a fight between us brothers. It was worry. We all ate quickly and quietly, none of us in the mood to talk.

When we finished, she brought our check over and Viper grabbed it before it hit the table.

"Gimme that," I said with my hand out.

"I got it," he swatted me away playfully. "You're gonna need me to pay for lunch for a while if you keep popping out kids the way you are."

Andy puffed his cheeks out trying to keep his laugh in, but was unsuccessful. He and Viper chuckled the whole way to the front podium to pay the bill, while I hung back at the table and fished around my pocket for the tip. I pulled out a bunch of bills, mostly fives and tens, but looked through them for the one hundred dollar bill I knew was in there. I finally found it and tucked it under a glass for the waitress.

A couple hours later as I sat facing my locker, I chugged the last of my apple juice and slammed the bottle down on the bench next to me.

"Jesus, Murphy. Calm down. What did that bench ever do to you?" Louie, my annoying teammate, joked as he walked behind me.

I didn't turn to look at him or even acknowledge his existence. I was too pissed off.

They'd just updated the weather report, and almost the entire state of Iowa was now under a blizzard warning. No way were they going to let our plane fly through that. We hadn't gotten the official word, yet, but I knew it was coming.

Desperate to tune the world out and focus on the St. Louis Blues offense that would be attacking my net within the next couple of hours, I put my earbuds in, turned AC/DC on and started re-taping the grip on my stick. Round and round my hand went as I willed my brain to concentrate on hockey and not snow, at least for the next few hours.

I felt someone sit down next to me and I looked to my right. Viper was staring straight ahead at his locker with a scowl on his face. I pulled my earbud out. "What's up?"

"Nothin'," he lied.

I knew Viper better than Viper knew Viper. "Liar."

"Fuck you."

"Alrighty then," I said with a laugh as I put my bud back in.

He reached over and plucked it out. "Sorry."

"Shut up, you're fine. What's going on?"

He shrugged. "You and Andy had your moments this morning. Now it's my turn."

"What? No!" Swinging my one leg over the bench, I turned toward him. "What happened to Viper Claus and you single-handedly saving Christmas if need be?" I smacked his arm with the back of my hand. "C'mon, man. Snap out of it. We need you on the ice today. The Blues are breathing down our necks in the division. We can't let them catch us."

"It's still early in the season," he mumbled

"It is, but how many seasons come down to a one or two game difference? Get your head out of your ass. Let's win this game and *then* you can sulk."

He took a long, deep breath, inhaling through his nose.

"You're right."

"Hell yeah I'm right! Now let's go!" I punched his arm hard and he looked over at me with a big smile.

"You're kinda dreamy when you're all excited like that, Murphy," he said as he gave me a wink.

"Ugh," I groaned as I stood. "Welcome back, dickhead." I put my earbud back in and let the music carry me to the start of the game.

Exactly two hours and twenty-four minutes later, we all walked back into the locker room with our heads hanging. We got the win, but it wasn't pretty. We played like shit and only won because the Blues played shittier. Every single guy on the ice, including the refs, and the few fans who braved the weather to show up at the arena, had their minds elsewhere. It was obvious that we were all preoccupied. Christmas Eve was the next day and as much as we liked each other as teammates, we didn't want to be with each other on that day.

We took our usual spots in the locker room and waited for Collins to come in and talk about the game, but when he walked through the door, something was different. He looked different; he walked different. The mood in the room shifted.

"So, I'm not gonna drag this out because I know we all want to get the hell out of here. No way is the plane going up in this weather. I'm sorry, guys. I know none of us want to be here tonight, but it is what it is." He cleared his throat and pushed his glasses back up his nose. "They're going to let me know if, and when, we can get a plane tomorrow, but even that's gonna be a stretch with this damn weather. All of you keep your phones on you, please. We'll be in touch with more news soon." With that, he turned and strode from the locker room just as upset as the rest of us were.

No one talked.

No one knew what to say.

We all knew it was coming, but it was still shocking when it did.

Some guys walked to the shower.

Some stood off in the corner on their phone.

Some just sat on the bench in a daze.

I rinsed off and threw my sweats back on, then walked over to my locker to pack up my things, thinking about Kacie and the girls the whole time.

How am I going to tell her this?

Her heart was going to sink and take mine right along with it.

I squatted down and began shoving my pads into my bag when Viper squatted down next to me and spoke quietly. "Don't say a fucking word to anyone, but pack up quickly. When we get back to the hotel, instead of going up to your room, hang around the lobby until everyone leaves."

I frowned at him. "What are you talking about?"

"We're leaving. Tonight."

"What? How the fuck are you going to make that happen?"

He stared back at me and arched one eyebrow as a sly smile moved across his mouth. "I'm Viper Claus, remember?"

Chapter 12

Michelle

AFTER SNOWMEN, S'MORES IN THE fireplace, and a shorter naptime than we would have liked, it was time for dinner. Kacie and Sophia had been cooking for us the whole week, so Darla, Dani and I got together and decided to surprise them and take over cooking and cleanup duty for the night.

"Wait, *you're* going to cook dinner?" Kacie said to me with wide eyes when I told her.

"No, I'm not, you brat." I smacked her arm. "Dani said I'm not allowed anywhere near the food, so I'm in charge of cleanup."

She giggled. "That's probably a good thing. I love you and all but you can't cook to save your life."

"Not only can't she cook to save a life, she'd probably *end* someone else's if she tried." Darla let out a hefty laugh as she filled the large pot with water and set it on the stove.

My mouth fell open as I turned and whipped the dishtowel

in my hand at the back of Darla's head. "You're a brat too!" Darla's shoulders shook as she laughed but didn't turn around.

"What are we having anyway?" Kacie asked as she sat at the island.

"We're making pasta and a big ol' salad. Oh!" I blurted, suddenly remembering the bread in the pantry. "I'm gonna cut the loaf of French bread while it's still good."

"What are we doing after dinner?" Darla asked.

I took a water bottle out of the fridge and slid it across the island to Kacie. "I don't know, but my kids barely had naps today so I'm hoping they're going to go down a little early. Tomorrow is Christmas Eve and I don't want them to be cranky little monsters."

A heaviness hung in the room as we exchanged awkward glances. I think we'd all been in denial that Christmas Eve was upon us and it was looking less and less likely that the boys were going to make it home.

Clearing my throat, I craned my neck and peeked over the couch at the kids. "I'm gonna go check on the little ones, I'll be back." I stood and walked into the family room, plopping down on the couch with the Emma and Becca. Lucy and Piper sat on the other couch with Grace and Maura snuggled up on their laps. "You guys are watching *The Grinch* again? Isn't it like the tenth time?"

"Shhh!" Emma said, putting her finger up to her lips.

"Sorry," I whispered. My eyes danced around the family room looking at all of Sophia's beautiful decorations. The most amazing thing had to be her tree . . . standing nearly fifteen feet tall and covered floor to ceiling in ornaments. I walked over to get a closer look. Sophia's tree looked more like a scrapbook than a tree, telling years of stories, memories, and accomplishments. Ornaments Kacie made as a kid with pictures of her toothless grin on them, handprints of the twins in hardened clay, a personalized toolbox ornament with Fred's name on it. I always knew Kacie was sentimental like her mom, but at that moment, standing in front of Sophia's tree, I got just *how* sentimental they both were.

Snowflakes glistening against the porch light caught my eye as they fell. I stepped to my right and moved closer to the French doors to get a better look. I cupped my hand around my eyes and leaned in against the glass to peek out and then let out a small gasp. The sparkling white and silver mounds flowed seamlessly over the deck, covering almost all of the deck furniture. Sophia's birdhouse that sat on the table had completely disappeared. My eyes lifted past the deck out to the yard. Each limb of each tree looked like it wore a thick, white sparkly sweater of snow and the lake no longer existed, looking more like a plain field instead. Though it was breathtaking to look at, I knew it was damn near impossible to fly in. My pulse quickened with anxiety as I turned from the window.

All of the girls were still gawking at the TV with their mouths hanging open, and I wasn't ready to go back into the kitchen just yet, so I decided to check on the boys. As I headed down the hall to the playroom, I could hear them cheering. I knocked softly on the door and pushed it open. "Hey, guys."

They both looked up from the board game they were playing long enough to smile and say hello.

"What are you guys playing?" I sat on the edge of the couch and leaned forward to try and see better.

"Monopoly," Logan said.

"Monopoly?!" I exclaimed. "Logan, you know Matthew's only six, right?"

Logan nodded.

"And this game is a little old for him and he might not fully understand it yet?"

Logan's eyes lifted to mine. "He's winning," he said dryly.

Matthew smiled proudly as he lifted his huge stack of fake cash in the air.

I laughed and sat back against the couch as I crossed my arms over my chest. "Well, then, carry on."

Logan picked up a card from the stack in the middle and read it out loud. "You have been elected chairman of the board. Pay each player fifty dollars." He groaned and picked up some of his play money, reluctantly handing it to Matthew.

"So, how come you two are hiding out in here rather than watching *The Grinch?*" I asked.

Matthew's eyes rose up to look at Logan who just shrugged. "I don't know," Logan said, "We've seen *The Grinch* a million times already . . ." He trailed off but I knew he wasn't saying something.

"And . . ."

"And . . . we kinda wanted a break from the girls for a little bit." His face snapped toward me to see if he was in trouble for saying that.

"I get it," I said softly.

His eyebrows rose and his expression was alarmingly like his father's. "You do?"

"Yep, I do." I repeated. "Michael is too little to be part of your team, so it's just you two big guys stuck in this house with a whole lotta girls."

"Yeah," Logan agreed. "Until dad and the other guys get home, then it'll be better." I pressed my lips together to keep to keep my mouth from opening and saying the words that would break his little heart right there in the playroom, but he sensed it anyway. "They're not gonna make it, are they?"

I peered from his blue eyes to Matthew's and back again. "Buddy, we don't know anything yet. Just think positive, okay?"

His shoulders slumped slightly as he looked down at the ground and nodded.

Ruffling his wavy blond hair, I stood and walked to the door, but turned back before I got to the hall. "I mean it . . . just say a little prayer and think good thoughts, okay? It's the season of Christmas miracles. Maybe that plane will take off after all."

Chapter 13

BRODY

Our plane isn't gonna be able to take off after all.

I SENT THE TEXT TO Kacie and set my phone down on the table in the hotel lobby, glaring at Andy. "I still don't get why we have to lie to them. Why can't we just tell them that we're going to drive home?"

Andy sighed and ran his hand through his hair. "Trust me, I wanna tell Dani, too. But he's kinda right, Brody. What if we tell them we're going to drive, and then something happens and we're not able to make it? Then they've had their hearts broken twice."

My phone beeped and I pinched my eyes shut tight. I didn't want to read whatever it was she'd just answered back, but I had to.

Kacie: For sure? Is that the final answer? What happens now? Do you try again tomorrow?

I could picture the panic on her face as she frantically typed those words out. It was frustrating for me not to tell her that we were at least going to try, but Andy had a point. I couldn't disappoint her twice. Plus, we didn't even know if we were going to have a car yet. Viper was trying to figure that out now.

> The plane is for sure not taking off. I'm so sorry, baby. I have no idea what's going to happen from this point on, but I'll let you know as soon as we hear something from Collins. Don't be too discouraged yet. Maybe we can get out tomorrow morning or something. I love you.

> **Kacie:** Maybe. I love you too.

Her text was short, but it said all that needed to be said.

She was heartbroken.

Deflated.

I knew she was upset, but there wasn't much I could do to help from St. Louis. If anything, all that text did was fuel my desire to get home to her.

"Where is he with that damn car?" I mumbled out loud, not really to anyone.

"What are you guys still doing down here?" A voice boomed.

Coach Collins was standing behind me when I turned around. "Hey, coach. We just haven't gone up to the room yet." I hated lying to coach but, unfortunately, that lie needed to be told. No way would he okay us leaving and driving home without the team. We could be in serious trouble for doing what we were about to do, but I was willing to take the repercussions if it meant getting home to my family. Glancing nervously toward the huge glass front doors of the hotel, I prayed that Viper didn't pull up just then.

"Yeah, hard to wind down after a game like that. And then this weather isn't helping at all." He turned his head and glanced at the shower of snow out the front door.

Go upstairs. Go upstairs. Go upstairs.

"Yeah, we'll head up soon, though." I tried not to say too much and prolong the conversation. He needed to leave before

Viper showed up and we were all screwed. Except Andy. He was allowed to do whatever the hell he wanted. Viper and me? Not so much.

"Alright, boys. I'm beat so I'm heading up." He patted my shoulder and walked off toward the elevator. Without moving my head, I slid my eyes over and followed him until he disappeared around the corner.

Andy leaned forward and rested his elbows on his knees, looking straight at me. "You might want to prepare yourself," he said in a low, quiet whisper.

"Huh?"

"While you and Collins were talking, I texted Viper to see what the hell was going on with the car and he said the place was packed and they were practically out of cars."

"Fuck!" I said as my head dropped against the back of the couch, feeling defeated.

"No, no. He got one, but he said there wasn't a lot to choose from and—" he stopped talking as a huge grin broke out across his face.

"And what?" I asked nervously.

He took a deep breath, letting it out slowly. "And we couldn't be mad at him."

"Are you kidding me? What did he get?"

He shook his head, "I have no idea. He wouldn't tell me but he's almost here, so pick up your shit and let's head outside."

I sighed as I stood and pulled my Wild beanie onto my head, slinging my bag over my shoulder. "When Lawrence Finkle tells you not to get mad, that's a bad, bad sign."

Andy laughed as we walked toward the front door and waited. The receptionist stood and twirled her hair around her finger, completely bored out of her mind. No one checking in, no one checking out. She'd probably be standing there like that for a few days.

I felt a slap on my chest and looked at Andy, who was looking past me out the front door. He motioned his head, "Look. Headlights. I can't imagine any other lunatic would be out in this."

I turned and squinted to see better, but between the snow and the thick frame of the door I couldn't make much out. "Let's head out," I said as I pulled the hood of my sweatshirt over my head.

We braced ourselves for the shock of the blistering cold and opened the door, holding our breath as the frigid air slapped us in the face. I finally got used to the wind and cracked my eyes open. "No fucking way," I said incredulously.

Pulling up to the curb was Viper—in a bright green Volkswagen Beetle, wearing a Santa hat as he hung halfway out the window, singing at the top of his lungs, "Here comes Viper Claus, here comes Viper Claus, right down Viper Claus lane!"

"Uh . . . this is a joke right?" Andy said as Viper parked the car and hopped out.

"No, it's not a joke." He walked around to the back and opened the trunk, "This was literally the last car they had and our only shot at getting home in time. Now, toss your shit in there, hop on my sleigh and let me fly your asses home."

Andy and I exchanged skeptical glances, but we didn't have any other options. "Rock, paper, scissors for shotgun?" I asked him as we dropped our bags in the trunk.

"You can have it," he said. "That crazy son of a bitch is hopped up on candy canes and adrenaline and he's gonna sing the whole way home. You sit up there with him, and I'll throw my earbuds in and sleep in the backseat."

I got in the car, closed the door and buckled my seatbelt before looking over at Viper, who was staring at me with a wild grin on his face. "Oh God. You're gonna drive me fucking nuts, aren't you?"

He wiggled his eyebrows up and down. "Five hundred fifty-eight miles to go!"

538 miles to go

"Seventy-one bottles of beer on the wall, seventy-one bottles of beeeeeeeer, take one down and pass it around—"

"Where are we?" Andy shouted over Viper's loud singing.

"Uh—" I looked down at the GPS on my phone, "—about twenty miles outside of St. Louis . . . a town called Chesterfield. Why?"

Andy sighed and looked out the window. "Just trying to decide if it would be a good town to dump his dead body in or if I should wait a little bit."

I looked out the window at the tunnel of snow the car was slowly crawling through. The headlights only lit up about five feet in front of us and we had yet to go faster than twenty miles per hour. "I don't know," I said to Andy. "At this rate he's going to tire out quickly and we're going to have to take turns driving, and three is better than two, so let's wait a little longer before we ditch him."

493 miles to go

We'd been in the car for three hours and only gone sixty-five miles. "This sucks," I groaned, suddenly glad that we didn't tell the girls we were leaving. At this rate, there was a chance we really wouldn't make it home before Christmas Day.

"Yep," Viper agreed. "It's hard to drive in this shit, and if I go any faster than twenty we lose traction and swerve all over the fucking place. Not to mention, when was the last time you saw another car? It's like a damn ghost town out here."

"I know, kinda creepy. And I think we lost Andy." I peeked into the backseat. Andy had rolled up a hoodie and was sleeping on it against the window, his mouth hanging open. "His mouth is open. Should I throw something in it?"

"Yes!" Viper growled. "I have a box of Red Hots in my bag. Grab them."

I bent down and picked up Viper's backpack from the floorboard, searching quickly for the box of cinnamon candy before Andy switched his position. Finally I found it. I ripped open the tab and pulled a couple pieces of candy out before unbuckling and turning around in my seat.

"Hold the car steady." I shot Viper a warning glare, "And don't kill me."

He rolled his eyes but didn't take them off the road. "Please. I probably need to go more than twenty miles an hour to kill you. At this rate, the best I could hope for would be a broken arm or maybe some internal bleeding."

Ignoring him, I pinched a piece of candy in between my pointer finger and thumb, aiming it like a dart at Andy's mouth. I cocked my hand back and let it go, hoping it would land on his tongue and eventually burn the crap out of it, waking him up. Instead, it did go into his mouth, but skipped the tongue all together and went straight down his throat. He sat straight up, his eyes snapping open and his hand at his throat as he coughed and choked.

Once he calmed down, he looked at me like I was insane. "What the fuck is wrong with you?"

I laughed and turned back around without saying anything.

"Where are we anyway?" he grumbled.

I checked the map again. "Uh . . . Eolia, Missouri."

"Did you just say areola? Because if you did, I'm fucking packing my family up and moving here." Viper laughed.

451 miles to go

"What do snowmen use to make snow babies?" Viper said through a yawn.

I frowned and looked over at him, "Huh?"

"What do snowmen use to make snow babies?" he repeated.

My eyes shot back to Andy, who shrugged. "I don't know,

Viper. What?"

"Snowballs." He let out a loud, slaphappy laugh.

I twisted in my seat and raised an eyebrow at Andy. "Think it's safe to leave him now?"

Chapter 14

Kacie

"SHHHHH! YOU'RE GONNA WAKE THE kids!" I scolded in a loud whisper, which only made Michelle and Dani giggle louder. Darla looked at me and rolled her eyes with a smile. She was buzzed, but not nearly as buzzed as the other two.

Once the kids went to bed and we heard from the boys that their plane was, in fact, grounded, Dani and Michelle started tipping the wine back.

Michelle stopped laughing suddenly and stared at Dani, "Okay, can we go back to this wedding thing. Have you guys even talked about it, Dani?"

She shrugged, staring down at her wine glass. "Kinda. It's weird. I think because we live together already, neither of us are in a huge hurry. It's not like life is gonna change once we're married."

"Psh!" Michelle blurted out. "You guys are still in the honeymoon phase of your relationship. You just wait."

"Wait for what?" Dani looked at her with wide eyes. "What's gonna change?"

I picked up a coaster and threw it like a Frisbee at Michelle's head. "Michelle, stop scaring her!"

"I'm not, I'm just being honest," she defended with a giggle. "Is it not true? Do things not change a little bit?"

"Well, sure . . . but that's kinda life," I said with a shrug. "Besides, you say it like it's a bad thing."

"What changes?" Dani exclaimed, obviously annoyed that we weren't answering her question.

"Number one—sex." Michelle took another sip of wine.

"Oh—" Dani shook her head quickly, "—Andy and I are just fine in that department. I'm pretty sure that won't change at all."

Michelle swirled her glass around and raised an eyebrow at Dani. "It will. I promise. Eventually, you'll be so damn tired, you'll starfish your way through the week."

I giggled as Dani's eyes darted from me to Darla, then back to Michelle. "Wait. Starfish? What is that?"

Michelle and I glanced at each other, each of us waiting for the other to speak up. "No way," I finally scoffed, "you started this with her, now you finish it."

With wide, anxious eyes, Dani looked to Darla for an answer.

Darla raised her hands defensively, "Don't look at me. I've never starfished a day in my life. In fact, I'm the anti-starfish. I'm the one slapping the starfishes to wake them and tell them to look alive."

"I swear to God, if one of you doesn't tell me what the hell a starfish is—"

"Okay, okay," Michelle interrupted. "So you obviously know what a starfish is, like the sea creature?"

Dani nodded.

"Well, basically, when you're really tired at the end of the day and he wants sex, and you're too tired . . . you just starfish it. Meaning you lay there and dream about your to-do list for the next day while he does whatever. Then you get to go to sleep."

Dani's mouth dropped open and her head jerked back. "Do

you guys really do that?"

"Are you kidding me?" Michelle rolled her eyes. "Viper would *live* in my vagina if he could. Sex with him is amazing, but exhausting. Sometimes it's like ugh . . . just do whatever and let me go to bed."

Dani's shocked and horrified expression made me laugh so hard my belly shook. "Have you done this too?" she asked me.

I shrugged, trying to calm my laugh. "On occasion, but usually only if I'm really drunk. I want to sleep when I'm drunk, so if I've been drinking and he lays me on the bed, it's like lights out . . . see ya tomorrow. I have to struggle just to stay awake until he finishes."

"So, since we're going there and all, can we please talk about finishing?" Michelle sat forward off the couch and set her wine glass down on the coffee table. "I'm serious. Are your boys crazy in that moment, or is it just Viper? Because he is *so* loud when he comes that sometimes I'm worried the neighbor is going to call the cops."

"Oh my God!" I blurted out as everyone, except Michelle, erupted in laughter. "We are *not* going there."

Michelle frowned. "Why not? I'm serious. We've talked childbirth, poop, and everything in between. Why not this?"

"Because as much as I love your husband, I don't want to picture his O face every time I look at him," I joked back.

Dani's hand flew up to her mouth but it was too late. Little droplets of wine sprayed out from in between her fingers, covering the side of my head. "I'm . . . so . . . sorry," she said through a cough as Darla handed me a napkin. Michelle, on the other hand, was laughing so hard she nearly fell off the couch.

I stood and walked to the kitchen to get a damp dishtowel and clean myself up while Dani followed me, still apologizing. "Kacie, oh my God. Really, I'm so sorry."

"Dani," I chuckled, "it's fine. Don't worry about it."

"What is going on in here?" Mom said playfully as she

appeared in the kitchen doorway with her hands on her hips.

I turned the sink on and stuck my finger under it, waiting for the water to warm up a little bit. "Well, we started getting a little silly, and then Michelle tried explaining what a starfish was to Dani and all hell broke loose."

Mom tilted her head to the side and pulled her brows together. "Starfish? What's that?"

With a grin on my face, I turned from the sink and peeked over the couch at Michelle. "Hey, Michelle!" I called out. "Mom wants to know what a starfish is. Care to come over and explain?"

The next morning—Christmas Eve morning—I rolled over to an empty bed and my heart ached. The bed at my mom's just wasn't comfortable and I tossed and turned all night, so instead I opted to sleep at my own house, but that wasn't easy either. Seeing Brody's side of the bed untouched and his pillows still smooth made my eyes well up. Over the last few days, he kept telling me to wait and see and think positive, but it was Christmas Eve morning and he was still in St. Louis. There was nothing positive about that. I grabbed my phone off the nightstand and opened it, praying I'd missed a message overnight saying he was on the way home.

My text box was empty.

Merry Christmas Eve. I miss you.

He answered a minute later.

Brody: Merry Christmas Eve. I miss you too. You just waking up?

Yeah. I slept over at our house last night.

Brody: Is everything okay?

Yeah, I just sleep better in my own bed . . . but I wish you were in it with me.

> **Brody:** I wish I were there too. Trust me. You smell a
> lot better than these two idiots.
>
> Any news on a flight?

I held my breath as those three little dots rippled across the
screen.

> **Brody:** No, baby. No news. I promise you'd be the first
> I'd call if we had a flight. So far . . . no plane.

Without answering him, I put my phone down, buried my
face in my pillow and sobbed. Shoulder shaking, breath hitching
sobs. One of those cries that lasts a long time, but makes you
feel so much better when you're finally done. I knew it wasn't
the end of the world and there were a lot of families who
couldn't spend Christmas together, but I just needed a few
minutes to get it all out. After I was done, I took a deep break,
took a quick shower and headed next door to the inn. Every
year, the girls and I made cookies for Santa on Christmas Eve
morning and I promised them, even with a houseful of people,
that wasn't going to change.

A few hours later, after all the kids had eaten, the kitchen had
been cleaned and it was time to bake.

"Okay," I clapped my hands together loudly, "who wants in
on this cookie thing?"

"Me!" most of the kids started shouting as their arms shot up
in the air.

Logan looked over at Matthew and nodded toward the hall.

"Wait, wait. What was that look about?" I asked. "You two
too cool to bake cookies?"

A mischievous grin spread across Logan's lips as he shook
his head. "Not bake, but we'll come back and eat them when
they're done."

"Oh, you will, will you?" I teased, swatting him with a
dishtowel before they both turned and hustled down the hall.

Lucy, Piper, Emma, Grace, Becca, and Maura stood in front of me with twitchy, anxious hands that were ready to work.

"You guys excited?" I asked.

They nodded like eager little baby birds sitting in a nest.

"Okay then. Let's get moving." Being in the kitchen with all those kids and seeing the excited looks on their faces was lifting my mood. I grabbed eggs, sugar, butter, and vanilla, and within seconds, the kitchen was a flurry of excitement and giggles. Thankfully my mom, Dani, and Darla all pitched in and took a station with a couple of the girls, while Michelle sat at the island and watched us, gently rocking back and forth as she nursed Michael.

The time flew by and before I knew it, we were loading cookie sheets into the oven and setting the timer. "We have too many cookies and not enough oven racks," I said as we closed the oven door. "We're going to have to cook them in several different batches, but boy will Santa be excited when he shows up here tonight."

Their eyes all lit up at the mention of Santa's name.

"Mama! Santa comes tonight?" Emma squealed.

I nodded.

Becca whipped around to Dani. "Does Santa know where we are?"

Dani nodded, her dark eyes smiling at Becca. "Yep. Remember when we mailed him your list? Well, we also added a note with the address here so he'd know where to find you."

"Okay, because I was really, really good this year and I don't want him to skip me." Becca pulled her hands up and scrunched up her face excitedly.

"Wait!" Lucy called out, turning toward me. "Santa is coming tonight? But Brody's not home yet."

"I know, honey." I walked over and put my arm around her, pulling her against me. "They're trying really hard, but no news on the plane just yet. Don't give up hope, though, okay? Airports are changing and adjusting all the time."

I wish I believed my own words.

"How about some tunes?" Dani called out as she grabbed the remote and turned the TV to the Christmas music channel.

"Jingle Bells" blasted from the speakers and it was like an instant adrenaline shot for the kids. I smiled to myself as they all started wiggling and shaking, holding hands as they danced around the kitchen.

"You need the boys for your dance party!" I called out over the music.

Piper gave me a big nod. "Get in line, girls! Follow me!" She shouted. The other girls fell in line right behind her, but the dancing didn't stop. They boogied and sang their way down the hall straight to the playroom. I waited for the yelling and resistance from the boys, but it never came. Instead, the line reappeared a few minutes later with Logan and Matthew strutting and dancing at the back of the line.

My heart soared. While the last month had been the most unexpected of my life, that moment right there—standing in the kitchen with my mom and best friends, watching as the kids marched and pranced in a big circle around the island with smiles on all of their faces and Christmas cookies in the oven—was one of the best moments of my whole life. It was one of those moments that I knew I'd remember forever.

Chapter 15

Viper

222 miles to go

THE SECOND MY EYES STARTED to get heavy, Brody kicked me out of the driver's seat and took over while I switched with Andy and napped in the backseat. A few hours later, I woke up to sunshine coming through the windows landing right on my face. I sat up and stretched my arms out as far as the tiny little matchbox car would let me.

"Where are we?" I growled.

"Just passing through Waterloo." Andy said. "And the sun is trying to come out. The roads are still total shit, but I'm starting to feel like we might just make this happen after all."

I rubbed my eyes and looked down at my phone. It was two o'clock in the afternoon.

"So we've been driving for what—like thirteen hours already?" I asked.

Brody huffed. "Driving is putting it loosely. A good part of the time you were sleeping, we just sat."

"Sat? Why?"

Andy turned and looked back at me. "There were a bunch of cars off on the side of the road in a ditch and the big plows were trying to get them out, so we had to sit and wait. Then we stopped for gas and a bite to eat."

"You fuckers stopped and ate without me?" I complained.

Brody chuckled and shook his head, "No, but we should have. You snore so damn loud. How the hell does Michelle sleep next to you?"

"Easy," I said nonchalantly as I looked out the window. "I give her so many orgasms before bed every night that she's exhausted and slips into a deep, peaceful slumber."

Brody looked over at Andy. "The shit he's shoveling is deeper than the snow."

I ignored him. "How long ago did you guys stop, anyway?"

"Why? You hungry?" Andy asked.

"No. I gotta piss, though. Bad." I turned to look and see if there were any cars behind us but there was no one on the road anywhere. "Here, just pull over."

"Right here?" Brody exclaimed.

"Yeah. I can't wait." I scooted over behind Andy's seat, my leg bouncing because I had to pee so badly.

Brody sighed loudly as he pulled the car off to the side just a little. "I'm not going any further into that deep snow on the side. We'll get stuck."

I nodded "Fine. Whatever. Just open the damn door."

The car finally came to a stop and Andy leaned all the way forward, pulling his seat with him.

"You're the best," I said to Brody as I squeezed out behind Andy. "I'll write your name in the snow as tribute."

I pulled my pants down, barely getting my dick out in time. As I stood peeing in the middle of what was most likely a corn field, somewhere in the middle of Iowa, out of the corner of my eye I saw the car start to pull away. "You're not fucking funny," I called out to Brody, unable to stop peeing. I took a big step to my left to try to stay with the car but it began moving faster. My junk bounced up and down as I started side-stepping quickly to keep up with it. "Knock it off, assholes!" The more I yelled, the harder they laughed. Finally I finished, tucked the Viking back into my pants and pounded on the back end of the quarter panel. The car stopped moving but they didn't stop laughing . . . for a long time.

153 miles to go

"I'm gonna call Gam real quick, just to say hello." I said as I scrolled through my phone looking for her number.

"Hey. Where *is* Gam this weekend?" Andy looked at me in the rearview mirror. "Did you invite her?"

I nodded and rolled my eyes. "I did, but she had other plans."

"Other plans?!" he repeated incredulously.

"Yeah. Her and Regina are spending Christmas with Phil and his brother."

Brody turned his head toward me. "Phil? Isn't that the guy she was . . . dating?"

"Yeah, I guess. I mean . . . I don't know. Do old people date? According to her, Phil is her *gentleman friend*." I rolled my eyes again at the ridiculousness of the conversation we were having. "And apparently Regina began—*dating*—Phil's younger brother, George, so they're all gonna be together for the holiday."

Looking back out the front window, Brody shook his head and laughed. "Kids these days are so cute."

"Hello?" Gam answered the phone.

"Hey, Gam. It's me."

"Lawrence! How are you?" Her voice rose with excitement.

"I'm . . . okay. How about you?"

"Well, looks like I might live to see another Christmas after all, so I'm fantastic. Why are you just okay?"

"It's been a long couple of days. Long story short, we had a few games and were supposed to be back at the inn by now, but the weather stepped in and gave us the middle finger."

"Oh, no!" she exclaimed. "I was watching it on the news and thinking about you. Are you stuck in St. Louis?"

I inhaled sharply. "No. But don't tell Michelle if you talk to her."

"What? Where are you?"

"We rented a car—"

"If that's what you can even call it . . ." Brody mumbled from the front.

"—And we're driving home. We've been in the car for like eighteen hours or something. I don't even know how long anymore. We're hungry, delusional and exhausted."

Silence from the other end of the line.

"Gam?"

She sniffed. "I'm here. I think that's the sweetest thing I've ever heard."

I frowned and rubbed my forehead. "What's sweet? Driving?"

"Yes, the whole gesture. Driving through this horrible weather to be home with Michelle and the kids for Christmas. All of you, frankly. You're good boys and I think it's sweet."

"You're getting soft in your old age," I teased.

"Screw you!"

"There's my girl!" I laughed out loud. "But seriously, are you sure you guys don't want to come to the inn for Christmas? Sophia makes a mean ham, and there's plenty of room for all of you."

"I appreciate it, Lawrence, but no. I'm going to stay home this year with Regina, Phil and George. Besides, this gives me a reason to stay alive and spend next Christmas with you guys."

I never knew a ninety-one year old's giggle could sound *that* adorable.

132 miles to go

We walked out of the gas station with turkey sandwiches that were God knows how old, but when you hadn't eaten in almost twenty hours, it tasted like Thanksgiving dinner. We sat in the car for a minute and ate them, washing them down with a nice cold Red Bull.

"Are you guys getting a little excited that we didn't tell them we're trying to get home?" I asked as I took another bite. "They're going to be so fucking surprised."

"I know," Brody agreed from the passenger seat. It was Andy's turn to drive for a while and I was happy in the backseat all by myself. "The only thing—" Brody glanced down at his phone and frowned, "—is that at this rate, they're probably going to be in bed by the time we get home."

"So we'll be sneaking in the house in the middle of the night on Christmas Eve? Holy shit! I really *am* Viper Claus!"

Andy popped the last bite of his sandwich in his mouth, crumbled up the paper and tossed it at me in the backseat. "You're more like an elf."

"Yeah, if elves were badass hockey players who solve problems like a boss." I gloated.

Brody nodded. "Ya know, I'm man enough to give credit where credit is due. You *did* jump in and solve this problem like a boss, Viper. Without your help, not only would this whole little sleepover at the inn thing not be happening, but we would be sitting in that hotel in St. Louis spending Christmas with each other instead of our families."

I leaned forward and peeked my head around the seat to look at him. "Awww, Brody Murphy. Are we having a moment? Wanna hop back here and consummate it with me?"

"Aaaaaand now it's ruined," Brody quipped.

106 miles to go

"Why did the snowman have a smile on his face?" I asked.

Brody and Andy sighed out loud in unison and I continued, "Because the snowblower was coming down the street."

Ignoring me, Andy turned and looked at Brody. "Would it be wrong to tie him to the roof for the last hundred miles?"

Chapter 16

Kacie

AFTER THE KIDS WERE ASLEEP, we set out all the presents and filled the stockings. It took us over an hour to place everything, and we had to move two couches out of the way, but it turned out perfect. I couldn't wait to see their faces in the morning. Once again, I decided to go back to my own house. And just like the night before, Fred wanted to walk me home.

"You don't have to do this," I said as I slipped my coat on.

He opened the front door for me. "I know I don't have to. I *want* to."

I smiled to myself when he reached out and held onto my arm as we walked down the wooden steps of the front porch. "You're cute, Fred, but I'm okay."

He turned his head toward me. "What? This," he motioned down at his arm. "I'm not helping you, you're helping me." We both laughed and made our way down the path he'd cleared toward my house.

"So things have been kinda crazy around here lately and I haven't had a chance to ask . . . how are things coming along at the new house?"

"Good," he nodded. "Great, actually. I think we'll be ready to move everything in there in about a week, right before the closing."

"I can't wait to see what else you guys have done to it." I meant it. They'd worked so hard and were so excited for their new adventure that I was starting to get excited too.

"Thanks, Kacie. I know it's meant a lot to your mom to have you so supportive and helping out over there. It's meant a lot to me too."

I glanced over and gave him a tight smile as he squeezed my hand. "I love you guys and I want you to be happy. Of course, part of me is sad about losing the inn, but you guys are more important."

"I have to be honest, I'm ready to let it go," he admitted softly, like it was a confession.

"Are you?"

"Yeah. It's been fun, but it's a lot of work. I'm ready for some down time with your mom. I want to wake up on Saturday morning and have coffee with her on our deck instead of running right outside to mow the lawn for three hours. And I want her to spend half an hour making dinner for two people instead of taking up half her day to make dinner for twelve. We're losing the inn but we're gaining so much time together. That means more to me than anything else."

A tear dripped from my cheek and landed on my coat as we walked up to the front of my house and I turned to face him, looking him right in the eyes. "Fred, you are the most amazing man and I'm so glad my mom has you. I'm excited you guys are going to have so much more free time too." I sniffed. "But you better still be planning on making those big dinners some of the time because I'm going to be bringing my gang over often, especially the further along I get in this pregnancy."

He let out a heartfelt laugh and I rose up on my tippy toes, planting a kiss on his scratchy cheek. "I love you, Fred. Good night."

"Good night, Kacie. I love you too."

I climbed the steps to my house and turned to watch him as he walked back through the woods to the inn one last time. Tears stung my eyes as I took a deep, shuddered breath and went in the house. I quickly changed into pajamas and climbed into bed with Diesel, falling asleep before my head even hit the pillow.

A soft thud woke me, but not enough for me to open my eyes. My ears were awake but my eyes felt heavy as sandbags, so I assumed it was Diesel hopping off my bed and going to his own in the corner.

Something soft ran along my arm and I sat up straight, my heart pounding wildly inside my chest.

Brody's beautiful grin was the only thing I saw in the moonlight shining through my window.

"Brody?" I choked out as I rubbed my eyes, not sure if I was really awake yet.

"Baby, it's me. I'm home," he said softly.

My eyes instantly filled with tears when I realized I wasn't dreaming. "You're home! What? How? I can't believe this." I held my arms out and he crawled across the bed toward me, hugging me tighter than he'd ever hugged me in our whole lives. "When did you land? Why didn't you call and tell me?"

"We didn't land," he mumbled into my shoulder, refusing to loosen his grip on me. "We drove."

"What? You drove? In this weather?"

He finally released me but didn't let go of my hands. "Yeah, took us a little over twenty-four hours."

"Wait," my head jerked back. "When we were texting and stuff yesterday . . . you were in the car?"

He nodded. "Don't kill me. We didn't tell you guys in case we weren't able to make it home for some reason. We didn't want to disappoint you twice."

"I'm not mad." I bit my lip, trying to contain the emotion I was feeling, but it was no use. Tears spilled out of my eyes as I stared into my husband's face. The face that made me smile every single day. The face that had been passed down to our daughters. The face I didn't think I'd been seeing for Christmas, yet here it was, sitting on my bed smiling back at me. "I'm so happy you're home, Brody. I take that back . . . there isn't a word big enough to describe how I'm feeling right now."

"Me too, baby. I can't wait to see the girls. I peeked in on all of them and it was so hard not to wake them and scoop them up."

"You saw the girls? Just now?"

"Yeah," he nodded, tucking a piece of hair behind my ear. "I thought you were over there, so that's where we went, and then your mom said you were here, so I ran through the woods as fast as I could."

"You ran?" my voice cracked.

"Are you kidding me? Those last fifty miles were the longest of my life. I couldn't wait to hug you." He took a deep breath and let it out, staring at me with his hypnotizing green eyes.

"Take your coat off, get under the covers and snuggle me, Murphy," I demanded. "I need your arms around me for at least three straight hours."

"Deal." He stood and yanked his coat and shirt off, climbing back in bed and hugging me from behind, scooting in as close as he could. "By the way, it looks amazing over there. Did it take you guys forever to set all that up? The presents fill the whole room."

"I know. I think we all went a little overboard, but we had fun."

I laced my fingers with his and pulled his arm tighter around me. After being apart for so many days and then thinking he wasn't going to make it home at all, I could not get close enough to him.

"Hey, Kacie?"

I turned my head just a little toward him but didn't say anything.

"It's twelve twenty-five in the morning."

"Yeah?"

"Merry Christmas, baby."

For the third time in fifteen minutes, my eyes teared up. "Merry Christmas to you, Brody Murphy."

Chapter 17

BRODY

*K*ACIE AND I SET OUR alarm to go off long before we knew the kids would be awake over at the inn so that we could be there when they ran down the hall and saw the mountain of presents around the tree.

We got up early, made love, took showers, made love again and headed out for our short walk through the woods, praying the kids were still asleep when we got there. I pushed the big wooden door of the inn open and we both froze.

Silence.

"Oh, thank God," Kacie said, breathing a sigh of relief.

"Kacie, it's barely five thirty in the morning, did you really think they'd be awake yet?"

"With these girls . . . you never know."

We walked quietly through the house and headed back to the kitchen. Sophia and Fred were sitting at the island with two cups of hot coffee in front of them, talking quietly with their heads close together.

"Merry Christmas!" Kacie said softly.

Sophia's head snapped towards us and it was obvious she'd been crying.

Kacie froze. Her smile dropped and her eyes zeroed in on her mom. "What's wrong?"

"Nothing," Sophia said as she shook her head quickly and wiped her eyes.

"Mom, don't lie. What's going on?" Kacie said, her tone growing more panicked.

"I promise, honey. It's nothing. I'm just having a moment." She cleared her throat and took a deep breath. "Reality is just starting to set in that I'll be handing over the keys to this place soon and I'm feeling a little emotional about it."

"Awwww!" Kacie's bottom lip shot out as she rushed over and wrapped both arms around her mom. "It'll be okay, Mom. I know it's hard to let go, but just think about how awesome your new place is and how much more free time you'll have."

Sophia sniffed again, letting out a quick laugh. "Look at this. I'm supposed to be the one comforting you, not the other way around."

Kacie squeezed her mom tight. "Yeah, well, maybe I've learned a few things over the last month or so."

"Daddy!" Emma squealed as she appeared in the doorway. The instant our eyes connected she broke into a full sprint and didn't stop until she was in my arms.

"Hi, baby girl!" I picked her up and squeezed her as hard as I could without hurting her.

She pulled back and looked at me. Her face was still puffy from sleep and her eyes were barely open but she lifted her tiny hands and cupped my cheeks. "I didn't think you were gonna be home in time."

"I didn't either, but me and Uncle Viper and Uncle Andy drove all night long and made it just in time."

Her eyes inspected my face as if to make sure I was really there. At that moment, I would've given anything to know what thoughts were swirling around in that little head of hers.

Suddenly, her eyes grew huge and her mouth fell open. She leaned forward and put her face so close to mine that our noses were touching. "Do you think Santa ate our cookies?" she whispered.

"I don't know. Should we go check?"

She nodded and we walked to the family room together.

On the coffee table was the big red plate that had little Santa faces painted all over it. For as long as I'd known her, Kacie only took that plate out on Christmas Eve and it only had one purpose. Santa's cookies.

As we got closer, Emma let out a soft gasp. "Daddy, look!" she pointed and squirmed to get out of my arms. I set her down and she rushed over to the table, leaning down for a closer look. The cookies on the plate were half eaten and crumbs were scattered on the table next to the plate. "Whoa! He was hungry!" she exclaimed.

"He's not the only one!" Viper bellowed as he walked into the kitchen, stretching his arms high above his head. He headed straight for Sophia and wrapped his big arms around her from behind as he kissed her cheek. "Merry Christmas, mama Sophia."

She planted a kiss on his cheek. "Merry Christmas to you, too, Viper."

"How'd you sleep?" I said to Viper as he walked toward me.

"What sleep?" he said, wiggling his eyebrows up and down. He held his hand out to me and I shook it as he learned in close, "The beds in those guest rooms squeak really loudly when you get movin,' huh? If we were paying to stay here, I would definitely owe Andy and Dani a free night."

I laughed and shook my head as Emma tugged on my hoodie to get my attention.

"When can we open presents, Daddy?" She looked up at me with impatient, eager eyes.

I rubbed her soft, pink cheek with the back of my finger. "Why don't you go wake the other kids?"

"But Gigi said I'm an early bird and that I should try and be quiet in the morning."

I shrugged. "It's Christmas. Go for it!"

Her mouth fell open for just a second before her lips morphed into a big grin and she took off down the hall, her little feet stomping against the wood floors as she ran.

"Santa came! It's present time!" she yelled when she got to the room. Within seconds, the kitchen was a chaotic scene of hugs and sleepy, excited faces. I stood in the family room, leaning against the back of the couch with my arms crossed over my chest as I took it all in. Lucy and Piper looked through the sea of people, finding me at the exact same time. They both ran over and crashed into me so hard that I almost flew backwards over the couch.

I put my arms around them and squeezed back, thinking they'd let go but they didn't. Kacie saw us and walked over, her eyes red-rimmed.

"Don't you guys want to open presents?" I said with a chuckle.

"We don't care about presents," Piper mumbled into my hoodie.

"We're just happy you're home" Lucy's voice shook.

I leaned back and tried to look down at her. "Are you crying, Lucy?"

She nodded, and I looked up at Kacie with a frown, wondering if I did something wrong. Her nose scrunched up and she grinned at me with a shrug. "Hormones," she mouthed.

I narrowed my eyes, glaring at her playfully. "Not funny."

It took over four hours to open all of the presents under the tree, and it included a thirty-minute break for breakfast because

Viper complained that he was wasting away to nothing. Sophia had made a breakfast casserole the night before and filled three crockpots with it. I had no idea crockpots were for breakfast, too, and honestly, it was a life game-changer.

After we finished, and wadded up wrapping paper had taken control of every corner in the room, the kids took their favorite presents and ran back to the playroom. Everyone except for Grace, who'd been glued to me since she saw me. I sat on the couch with her resting against my chest.

"She's kinda in love with you today, huh?" Kacie stared at us with a look in her eyes. I don't know what that look was called but I'd seen it many times. It was that loving look a mother gets when she finds something sweet in the simplest of moments.

"Yeah, she is . . . and I'm eating it up for as long as I can." I put my hand on Grace's back, feeling it rise and fall with each breath.

Sophia walked into the room with a big tray full of different Christmas mugs and set it on the table. "Some are coffee, some are hot chocolate. Take whatever you'd like."

Viper passed out mugs to Michelle, Dani, Darla, and Kacie first, then looked over at me. "What do you want, brother?"

I shook my head quickly. "Nothing right now, I'm good. Thanks."

"So what's the plan the rest of the day?" Viper asked as he sat back in his chair and took a sip of coffee.

Fred lifted his hands in the air, holding them open to the room. "I think you're looking at it. Keep the fire burning in the fireplace, watch a little football, maybe take a nap at some point."

"Sounds good to me," Viper agreed. "Especially the nap part."

"I'm sure you boys must be exhausted." Sophia shook her head. "I still can't believe you drove for an entire day to get here. You're all pretty amazing."

Viper puffed his chest out, "I'd just like to remind everyone, once again, that it was all Viper Claus' idea."

"Viper Claus?" Kacie giggled. "That's kind of adorable."

"Oh, God. Don't." I looked over at her. "Don't encourage him. We had to listen to him refer to himself as Viper Claus in the third person almost the whole way home."

"I would say that being in a car with Viper for an entire day is the equivalent of traveling alone in the car with . . . ten two-year olds," Andy teased. "When they're awake and chattering, your blood pressure is raised, and then when they finally fall asleep, you try not to make any sudden movements or sounds and wake them up."

Everyone in the room laughed out loud, even Viper.

"Well, I appreciate you guys putting up with Viper Claus and fighting so hard to get home. I honestly cannot imagine sitting here right now without the three of you with us." Kacie said as she scooted over and tucked herself into my side.

"There's something else I'd like to say real quick, if that's okay . . ." Sophia sat up straight and cleared her throat. "Several years ago, my life was very different. It was just Kacie and me here with the girls—and Fred—who didn't have a twinkle in his eye for me yet. Then one weird rainstorm came along and flooded out the whole county, which led to Brody staying here for a few days. What I learned over this time is that you really have no idea how much *one day* can change your life. I didn't know it at the time, but that one day, and that one rainstorm, brought me an amazing son-in-law who I love like my own, two—soon to be three—more grandbabies to love, a wonderful husband who loves me more than I've ever been loved in my life, and all of you guys, who have become not only Kacie's extended family, but mine as well. I'm just so thankful for all of you . . . and for this last week you chose to spend here with us— " She pinched her lips together and shook her head, unable to talk anymore.

The whole room was quiet, everyone dealing with their emotions in different ways. The girls were teary-eyed; Andy stared down at his mug. Even Viper was choked up—which was about as rare as an eighty degree Christmas day in Minnesota.

I let out a heavy sigh and raised my mug in the air. "I'll drink to that . . . to the Cranberry Inn gang."

Chapter
18

Kacie

AFTER DINNER, THE BOYS ALL stretched out on the couches and floors in ham comas. Darla, Michelle, Dani, and I sent my mom away so that we could take over cleaning duties since she single-handedly prepared the whole Christmas dinner.

"I swear, in her last life, your mom was a master chef or something," Dani said as she scrubbed the sweet potato casserole dish that was too big to put in the dishwasher.

"I know, right?" Michelle agreed. "I'm over here just trying to not burn water when I boil it and your mom whips together a seven course meal like it's nothing."

"Why do you think Brody sneaks over here for leftovers all the time? I can hold my own in the kitchen, but not when compared to her." I laughed.

Andy walked up to Dani at the sink and wrapped his arms around her waist. "Can I steal you for a second?"

"Uh . . . yeah, give me a minute to finish this," she answered.

Darla took the dish from her, "Go. I got this."

"Thanks." Dani smiled at her and took Andy's hand as he

pulled her from the room.

I frowned and looked from Dani to Darla to Michelle. "What's that all about?"

Michelle popped an olive from the dish into her mouth. "Not sure. I think he's giving her his Christmas present."

"Ah, got it." I said.

"Did Brody get you anything?" Michelle asked.

"I don't think so, but I don't even care. Him planning this whole week, then driving home yesterday and stuff . . . that's present enough for me." I shrugged.

My cell phone rang from the counter. I glanced down at it and smiled to myself.

"Hey!"

"Hey! Merry Christmas!" Zach said cheerfully.

"Merry Christmas to you, too! Were you up early?"

"Yeah, but not for presents. The upside to having a six-month old at Christmas is that she has no idea it's Christmas so we can sleep in. The downside is that she's teething and was up at four o'clock. I'm beat."

"Awww, poor baby. Teething sucks!"

"It does."

"I wish you guys could have made it today," I said sincerely.

"I know, and Claire said thank you for the invite, but her parents came in to spend Christmas with the baby, so we were obviously trapped."

I let out a quick giggle. "Next year. Anyway, want to talk to the girls?"

"Yes, please. And tell Brody and your mom I said Merry Christmas."

"I will. Same to you, Claire, and Audrey. Hang on one sec . . ." I put my hand over the phone and called out, "Lucy, Piper!" They ran down the hall, stopping on a dime in the kitchen doorway.

"Yeah?" Piper said.

"Daddy Zach is on the phone." I stretched my arm out and handed the phone over. Piper took it and disappeared down the hall, rambling things off to her dad as fast as she could.

"Kacie. You're amazing," Michelle said with a heavy sigh.

I spun and looked at her, trying to figure out where that came from. "Huh?"

"Your relationship with the girls' dad just blows me away. With everything that happened, no one would blame you if you wanted to be bitter and hate him forever, but you guys not only co-parent seamlessly, you actually get along. It's just . . . refreshing."

"Thanks," I said as my face flushed. "I'm not gonna lie, it wasn't always like this. There was a while at the beginning where I was resentful and bitter, but then I took a step back and thought about it. I feel like the more people that love my girls, the better, right? So why try to block what could be a really positive relationship for them? It took some time, and a lot of tongue-biting, but eventually we learned to work together. Once we had that down, the friendship bloomed. We're not super tight best friends or anything, but I know that he and Claire will be sitting next to Brody and me at their weddings one day with genuine smiles on our faces. I can't think of a better gift for them."

Darla stared at me with a deadpan expression on her face.

"What?" I asked defensively.

"Nothing," she shook her head back and forth slowly. "Your maturity is just off the charts sometimes. If I were you, I'd have a whole line-up of Zach voodoo dolls in my room. A summer one, a winter one, a pajama one . . ."

"Stop it," I laughed as I threw a dishtowel at her.

"Who's Lucy talking to?" My mom asked as she came into the kitchen.

"Zach," I answered. "He called to wish them Merry

Christmas. Said to wish you and Brody one too."

Mom stretched her neck up high and glanced over the couches into the family room. "Speaking of Brody . . . where is he?"

I followed her stare and looked for him too. "No idea," I said.

"He left here about half an hour ago," Fred answered. "Said he'd be back soon. He had to go to your house for something."

I rolled my eyes. "He's probably hiding in the bathroom again."

Just then, I heard the front door slam shut and Brody walked through the kitchen. His solid black beanie was pulled down low, making his eyes look greener than normal and his cheeks were pink from the cold.

"Hey! We were just talking about you. Were your ears ringing?" I teased.

He smiled at me and those dimples I love so much made an appearance. "Sophia, can you keep an eye on the girls for a minute? I want to show Kacie something."

"Sure," she agreed.

His eyes returned to mine. "Put your coat and boots on. Meet me on the front porch, okay?"

I narrowed my eyes and stared at him skeptically. "Okay?"

"Just do it," he said with a laugh, then bent down and kissed the tip of my nose.

I slipped my boots on and bundled up in my coat and hat as I wracked my brain trying to figure out what that boy was up to. He was sitting on the porch swing when I opened the front door. What little sun we'd had started to go down already and it was starting to turn dark.

"What are you doing, you crazy man?" I said as I stepped out and closed the door behind me.

"I want to talk to you for a minute without anyone else around." He stood and walked over, taking my hands in his. "I feel terrible because I never got a chance to go shopping and get you jewelry or something pretty for Christmas."

I tilted my head to the side. "Brody, you should know by now that I don't care—"

"Wait," he cut me off. "Let me finish." He took a deep breath. "I did something a few weeks ago and was waiting for the perfect time to tell you, and I feel like this is it."

My eyes started dancing around the porch, trying to figure out what he was talking about. "Okay?"

"Follow me," he said excitedly.

He took my hand and led me off the porch and around the inn, giving me a major case of déjà vu. "Brody, slow down! The snow is too high and my legs are short!" I giggled, trying to keep up with him as we marched through the snow together. Halfway through the yard, I finally looked up and around him. "What the—is that a Christmas tree out there?"

"Just keep walking," Brody ordered.

Finally we got to the edge of the pier and he stepped back, holding his arms out wide. "Ta-da!"

"Ta-da what?" I still didn't understand what was going on.

"Come here," he took my hand again. We walked to the huge, brightly lit tree at the end of the pier and he stopped and looked at me. "When I was trying to think of what to get you for Christmas, I kept coming up empty, Kacie. You're a simple, low maintenance girl who doesn't like a lot of fancy frills so I was stressing about it. Then I got to thinking. What matters most to you . . . and that was easy. Your family."

I nodded slowly, growing more confused by the second.

"But not just your family. You're all about memories and preserving memories and making memories, so when I found out your mom was selling the inn, I knew I couldn't let this pier go."

My heart started racing. "But how? It's on the inn's property."

A sexy little grin grew across his mouth. "Correction, it *was* on the inn's property, but it's on the very edge of the property line, almost on ours. So when I found out she sold it, I called her realtor who put me in contact with the buyer's lawyer. After some haggling back and forth, and an offer they couldn't refuse, we had the county come out and redo the property lines, so we now own this whole section . . . and this pier. *Our* pier. The pier that we had our first non-date on, the pier we've made love on, the pier I proposed to you on. No way was I going to let someone take that from us, so I bought it."

"This pier is ours now?" I squeaked out.

"Yep," he nodded. "And we can do whatever you want with it. Leave it here, move it to our backyard. Whatever you want to do I'm fine with—"

I crashed my mouth against his. Never in my life had I needed to kiss him more than I did at that exact second. This man, this husband of mine, knew me better than I knew myself. Buying the pier never crossed my mind, but as soon as he said it, suddenly I couldn't imagine my life without it officially being ours.

"Brody Michael Murphy," I said breathlessly as I pulled back. "I don't know what I did to deserve you, but you are *the* most amazing man in the whole world, and there are days I still can't believe you're mine."

"So I guess you like the pier?" He dipped his head, trailing soft kisses down my neck.

"I don't like it, I love it. Thank you for being *so* thoughtful." His mouth lingered, gently licking my skin and making certain parts of my body come warm up very quickly. "I swear, if there wasn't a houseful of people up that hill right now, I'd make you make love to me right here, right now."

"Uh—" he laughed quickly and lifted his head, "—even if the house was empty that probably wouldn't happen. Little Murphy isn't exactly a fan of the cold. He kinda hides when we're outside in the winter."

I raised on eyebrow at him. "We've been having sex for six

years now, so I consider myself an expert on your body, and I promise you . . . *Little* Murphy is not an accurate description."

He laughed again and rubbed his hands up and down my arms quickly to warm me up. Then he pulled me in tight against his chest and rested his chin against the side of my head as he looked out over the lake. "Kacie Murphy. I love you. I love you a whole hell of a lot."

"I love you right back, number thirty."

"Wanna head inside? It's getting cold out here."

"Yeah," I said with a sigh. "Since everyone is leaving first thing in the morning, the girls said they're going to start packing up tonight. I should probably help them."

I sniffed as I turned to head back up the pier, but he held onto my hand and tugged me back. I looked up at him and he nodded his head once to the side, flashing that million-dollar grin. "One more time . . . pay the toll."

I couldn't stop the smile that involuntarily crossed my lips when he said those words to me. "Gladly."

Epilogue

BRODY

I GLANCED UP AT THE clock.

One minute.

One fucking minute to go and we would win the Stanley Cup. My heart was in my throat and I was using my adrenaline to keep the puke at bay. Every muscle in my body was tense and I focused as I hard as I could on that little black puck.

48 seconds.

The guys and the puck were moving fast and fierce across the ice. Every player on the Tampa Bay Lighting was as focused and desperate as I was, but this was it.

28 seconds.

They skated toward me and my eyes zoned in on the puck as they passed it back and forth. The center came in and screened me on the left side to try and obstruct my view as the defenseman shot the puck from the top of the circle. Moving to the left to get a view of the puck, I jerked my hand up and caught it at the last second just before it flew past me.

19 seconds.

I handed the puck off to Louie and prayed harder than I'd ever prayed in my life. I prayed for Louie to keep control of the puck and not lose it. I prayed for those last seconds to go by quickly. I prayed to be a hero to the team I loved so much.

3 seconds.

2 seconds.

1 second.

The buzzer sounded, and almost immediately the shrill noise gave way to the cheers from the crowd. It was deafening. The whole building shook. My arms flew in the air as I threw my mask off and tossed my stick down. Every member of the Wild skated toward me, all of us colliding into each other in a hornet's nest of hugs and celebration. The guys from the bench hopped over the boards and skated over to us as well. Coach Collins ran out onto the ice with tears in his eyes. For the first time ever—*ever*—the Minnesota Wild were the Stanley Cup Champions!

I immediately looked through the mess of jerseys for Viper and found him looking for me, too. We got razzed on social media and in the news for our 'bromance' but in that moment, I didn't give a shit. I needed to hug my best friend. We locked eyes and crashed into each other.

"We did it! We fucking did it!" Viper screamed as we hugged. "Congratulations, brother!"

I squeezed him harder than I ever had in my life. There is no one I would rather have on my team, both on the ice and off. The Tampa Bay Lighting players waited patiently, with disappointment across their faces, for our celebration to end so the handshake line could begin.

"Guys! Guys!" I called out as loud as I could. "Handshakes!"

We put our celebration on hold and fell into line, skating past each player of the Tampa Bay Lightening, shaking hands and showing our respect as we went. They wanted it just as badly as we did, but the win fell in our column that night and for that I would be forever grateful.

After the Lightning players left the ice, the ceremony was

back on. The red carpet had been laid out and the podium sat empty at the end of it, waiting. The music began and a lump formed in my throat. Tradition was about to take over and I couldn't believe we finally got to be part of it.

"Ladies and Gentlemen," the announcer boomed. "The Stanley Cup!"

Phil Pritchard and Craig Campbell, wearing navy blue blazers and white gloves, slowly walked down the tunnel carrying the thirty-five pound Stanley Cup statue. They continued down the red carpet and out to the stand, where they set the polished silver trophy down and walked back. The next few minutes were a blur as the announcer talked and the trophy was presented. I narrowed my eyes and frantically searched the families for my people, but everyone was jumping up and down and I couldn't find Kacie.

"Brody!" Coach Collins called my name and my head snapped toward him. "C'mon! Take Lord Stanley for a spin!"

I skated over to the trophy and took a deep breath. I'd dreamed of hoisting that cup above my head and skating around the rink with it just like so many before me had since I was a little kid . . . and now I was about to do it. I gripped both sides firmly, thanked God for all of my blessings, and lifted the three foot tall cup high above my head.

The crowd roared and people started taking pictures as I skated around for my victory lap with the Stanley Cup. My eyes teared up and I was torn between weeping with happiness and busting right through a brick wall from excitement. I yelled and cheered as I slowly skated around the rim of the rink. When I got to the other side where the families sat, my eyes searched for my family.

Finally, I found them!

Kacie cheered, jumping up and down when she saw me.

"You did it, baby!" she screamed out over the crowd with tears streaming down her face.

"*We* did it!" I yelled back.

Lucy, Piper, and Emma stood next to her in their Wild jerseys, pumping their arms up and down. On the other side was Sophia, who held a pouting Grace in her arms. Grace was never a fan of the games and the crowd noise, so she spent the whole game frowning with her fingers in her ears. Next to Sophia stood Fred, who looked as proud as I'd ever seen him with his chin held high. Baby Fred slept soundly in his arms, wearing his own customized Wild jersey with our last name on the back and the tiniest pair of noise protection ear muffs I'd ever seen. He was only three weeks old and had no idea what was happening, but it was a moment I couldn't wait to tell him about when he was older.

My parents stood behind Kacie and, of course, my mom was sobbing. Dad and my sister, Shea, were hugging and jumping up and down. Shea followed along as I skated for a bit, taking as many pictures as she could. When I got back to the center, I handed the cup off to Viper for his turn around the ice.

The whole team spent the next hour celebrating with the cup, taking pics and hugging each other. Finally, it was time for our families to come down. Kacie practically jogged along the red carpet, straight into my arms.

"Holy shit, Kacie. We did it! We actually fucking won!" I called out as I hugged her.

She squeezed me back hard. "I'm so proud of you, Brody!"

"Daddy! High five!" Emma yelled from below us.

I let go of Kacie and scooped Emma up. "Forget the high five, give your daddy the biggest hug ever!"

She giggled and then groaned when I gripped her tiny body.

"Can you believe all this craziness?" I said to Kacie, leaning down around Emma.

She shook her head slowly, staring up at me with her shimmering green eyes. "This is insane, Brody. I mean look at this crowd! Not one person has left the arena yet."

She was right; the stands were still packed full. Minnesota had waited so long to see the Wild win a Stanley Cup that clearly the fans were staying until the party was over and security kicked them out.

"Emma! Let's wave, okay?"

Emma nodded and we turned to the crowd. I pumped my fist high in the air and Emma waved to the crowd, beaming as if she'd scored the winning goal herself.

"How about a family photo?" the team photographer called out. "Maybe standing around the cup?"

I turned back and nodded at him.

Kacie took baby Fred from big Fred and I set Emma down so that I could pick up Grace. We gathered around the cup and smiled for a picture.

"Wait a minute, wait a minute," Viper called out as he walked over and carefully took the cup off the stand, setting it on the red carpet. "Not many people get to do this, so you're going to. Put Fred in there," he said to Kacie as he pointed at the top of the cup.

Her eyes grew wide and she looked at me nervously. "Am I allowed to do that?"

I leaned down close so she could hear me, "Hell yes! It's a once in a lifetime opportunity. Go for it!"

She bit her lip and nodded as she very gently lowered Fred into the top of the cup. We all leaned in around him and the photographer snapped a bunch of shots.

He pulled back and looked down at his camera. "That one's a winner for sure! Thanks!"

"Can I see it?" I asked.

"Of course!" he turned the screen toward me with a smile. My breath caught when I looked down and I was completely overcome with emotion. A tear dripped from my eye as I stared down at the two-inch by two-inch screen. As a kid, my only dream was to play hockey and win the Stanley Cup, but then I grew up and met Kacie and my dreams shifted just a little bit. Looking down at that picture of my wife, my daughters, my son, and the Stanley Cup all together in one shot, I realized that my new dream was simple.

I had the wife of my dreams, the kids of my dreams, and the career of my dreams, and all I needed to do for the rest of my life was make sure *their* dreams came true . . . though, one more Cup wouldn't hurt either.

The Bittersweet
End

A Note from
Beth

Wow! That's really all I can say at this point…wow! When I decided to start this little writing journey almost 4 years ago, I really never expected anyone other than my mom to buy and read my book. I certainly never expected so many of you to fall in love with Brody, Kacie and the rest of the Cranberry Inn gang and follow them along for seven books!!! Thank you. From the very bottom of my heart…thank you. For supporting me, for helping make my wildest dreams come true and most importantly, thank you for loving these characters as much as I do. While I'm sad to say good-bye to them, I'm ready to meet some new people and hear what they have to say to me. I hope you're as excited as I am!

Acknowledgements

The the amazing people who contributed to this book—Letitia Hasser, Tami Norman and Holly Malgeri. I am a hot mess of epic proportions almost all of the time. This book would not have been possible without your patience and understanding and incredible talents! Thank you so much for all of your help, and for not blocking me on Facebook. ☺

To all of my author friends, the FTN girls, and my COPA sisters—This job can be a very lonely one. Most days (as I'm sure most of you understand) can be pretty isolated as we talk to imaginary people in our heads and spend our days typing away. Most of you live all over the world, but knowing you're out there, always ready to listen and cheer me on makes life a little less gloomy. Thank you for being there to keep my company when I'm at my loneliest and for pushing me when I need it most.

To my Roomies—GAH! I don't even know where to begin with you guys. I seriously cannot imagine my life without every single one of you. Thank you for putting up with my random craziness in our little corner of Facebook, and for loving me—and my family—as much as you do. It means the world to me and I hope you stick around for a long, long time!

To my amazing friend, Pam Carrion—You are the peanut butter to my jelly, the yin to my yang, the Smokey to my Craig. I could write an entire book about how unbelievably awesome you are, but anyone who's lucky enough to be your friend already